The Greek Constellations - Aries

The Greek Constellations - Aries

Stephan De Jonghe

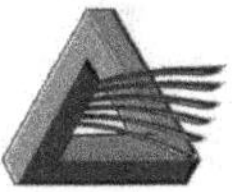

Contents

Copyright   vii
Cover   ix
The dedication   xi
Special thanks   xiii
Authors note   xv
Chronology   xvii

1 The constellation - Aries.   1

Novella one - the constellation Pisces   133
Novella two – the constellation of Capricorn   135
Novella three - Saturn's moon Pandora   137
Novella four - the constellation Taurus   139
Novella five - the constellations Scorpio   141
Novella six - the constellation Aries   143
Novella seven - the constellation Ophiuchus   145
Novella eight - the constellations Cancer and Leo   147
Novella nine - the constellation Gemini   149
Novella ten - the constellations Virgo and Libra   151
Novella eleven – the constellation Aquarius   153
Novella twelve – the constellation Sagittarius   155
Novella thirteen – the constellation Centaurus   157
The other Greek constellations   159
Follicle Farm – A novel adventure   161

Your concise guide to the meaning of life 163

Copyright

The Greek Constellations – Aries

Copyright © 2024 by Stephan De Jonghe

For permission requests, write to the
publisher at: stephansfolliclefarm@gmail.com

Ordering Information:
Special discounts are available on quantity purchases by book resellers, corporations, associations, and others.
For details, contact the publisher at the email address above.

The Greek Constellations – Aries by Stephan De Jonghe

ISBN 978-1-7636516-2-3 (paperback)
ISBN 978-1-7636516-3-0 (e-book)

Publisher
Stephan De Jonghe Publishing,
Hillarys, Perth, Western Australia,
Australia 6025

Printer and distributor
Ingram Content Group
1 Ingram Blvd.
La Vergne, Tennessee USA 37086

Cover

In the footsteps of Homer and Hesiod.

From Astronomy to Mythology

How the constellations came to be named by the Greek God's.

Stephan J De Jonghe

Novella Six

The constellation Aries

The story of Chrysomallos and Helle.

The dedication

To say that my darling wife is the love of my life
is an understatement.

Deb is my best friend, soul mate, confidant, and life partner.

Among so many other things, we also share a love of books, and
we have a massive library on display in our home of books that we
want to read.

Our topics include action, comedy, romance, science fiction,
crime, thrillers, and adventure.
We also have an impressive non-fiction collection.

My endeavours as an author represent a passion that burns
powerfully for me. I am driven to write.

I have many stories to tell, and writing them and publishing them
is my way of contributing to other people's library's.

Writing involves many hours of research and then sitting in soli-
tude, slowly assembling the words that details a journey into a read-
able story. One that was only previously an idea.

This takes a lot of patience and persistence.
After the story is put down, the process of editing begins.

Few non-writers understand that this stage can take as much five times longer than it takes to write the actual first draft.

My Deb gives me the support that I need to execute my writing passion.
She not only supports my writing, but also enjoys reading the stories.

Her assistance with proof reading, feed-back on content, and editing, is invaluable.
Especially after I've become blind to my own errors.
She understands how important it is to me and to you, the reader, to get it right.

I dedicate these books to my wife as my thanks to her for her on-going support,
and for her contributions to the finished publications.

We are a team.

We both hope that you enjoy this series of books,
and we look forward to your feedback.

Stephan and Deb De Jonghe

Special thanks

My special thanks go to Janey Emery – Renowned Australian artist, for giving me permission to use her art for the covers for my Greek Constellation series of books.

I hope you enjoy her art and the story within these pages.
Stephan De Jonghe - Author

Janey's Story - Born in Narrogin, Western Australia, Janey Emery's interest in art began as early as 2 years of age and led to art becoming the central element in Janey's Childhood. Excelling in art throughout her school years Janey devoted herself to the art course provided by Balcatta Senior High school, where her passion for art only intensified.

Janey has been painting fulltime since 1991 and has attained a high degree of respect in the art world from peers and art lovers alike. Janey has won numerous distinguished artistic awards for her work and has sold many paintings throughout Australia and overseas. Janey Emery is achieving the recognition her distinctive artistic talents deserve.

Janey is Self-Taught in All Mediums with the exception of leisure courses undertaken in oil and water colours.

Art has always played a part of who I am. From early childhood to now there has been a need for me to express myself through drawing and painting. I find peace in my craft, and I hope I bring that to my paintings.

To me, my Art is like breathing. Painting is my life.
Janey Emery

https://www.janeyemery.art/

Authors note

This story is based on Greek mythology. Aries however, is Latin (Roman) for a Ram. Many thousands of years ago, the origin of the constellation Aries was one of the stories imagined by ancient travelers and sailors.

Many of these stories owe some of their earlier history to the Phoenicians, Babylonians, and Mycenaean's, and were initially used to help ancient travellers remember star patterns as a nighttime navigational tool. Over time, these fascinating stories were greatly embellished on how the constellations came to be formed. The ancient Greeks called these constellations the "Katasterismoi" meaning, "the placing of the stars." They gave names and told stories about forty-eight out of the eighty-eight constellations that are recognised by the International Astronomical Union.

These mythologies were embellished as they were countlessly re-told with tales of gods encountering wild creatures, fighting fierce battles, and of course having lots of sex. After all, these men were away from home for lengthy periods of time. They shared these stories to entertain urban dwellers that they encountered, and from there the stories became legends, and for many people they became their religion.

A Greek poet and storyteller named Homer, was the first person to document these stories and he is most famous for the "Iliad" and the "Odyssey" which he composed some 2,800 years ago. Whilst very little is known about Homer, he is regarded by many as the founder of modern literature. His two main works were the first literary works to be taught formally to students. Interestingly, there are thirty-three film adaptations of the Odyssey, proving his works are still relevant to modern audiences.

Later, a poet named Hesiod, significantly contributed to Greek mythology and followed on from Homer's work. Together they are attributed with establishing ancient Greek religious customs, formal astronomy, the development of structured learning, documenting events, early economics, commercial farming, and time keeping.

The word "zodiac" originated from the Greek words "Zodiakos kuklos," meaning "circle of little animals". It wasn't until 50BCE that the first classical zodiac depicting the twelve astrological star signs in their current order was first depicted. It is known as the "Dendera zodiac."

During the 2nd century CE, a Greco-Roman astrologer and astronomer named Claudius Ptolemy worked on his documented Tetrabiblos into what is regarded as western astrology's primary source document and remains largely in use today. Also of note is that astronomers have named a crater on the Luna surface, and another on the surface of the planet Mars Ptolemaeus, in honour of Ptolemy and his contribution to astronomy.

The connection between Greek names and Roman names for the same deities came from their translation from one language to the other. In ancient Greek, Zeus is pronounced Dias. In Latin that became Djous Pater (Sky father) or Luppiter. In English this became Jupiter. Many names evolved in this way.

As an author, my goal is to turn what is known of the mythology, into an enjoyable story for today's reader.

Stephan J De Jonghe

Chronology

Yet another note from the author, Stephan De Jonghe

My "from astronomy to mythology" series of novellas posed some difficulties in terms of writing the stories into a logical chronology. Until the Iliad, and the Odessey, no one had ever written any of the tales of titan's forming the world, or their ultimate defeat by the gods who eventually resided in Mount Olympus. These stories were imagined piecemeal, embellished, refined, and retold over a thousand-year period. Unlike history, which did happen on a linear timeline and can be plotted, the timeline used in fictional stories were not relevant, and by their very nature at the whim of the story teller. Over the millennia, re-tellers of the stories frequently added details, and characters that were often inconsistent with the other stories. No one knew and no one cared, as they were mostly just for entertainment.

For the more serious devotees, these stories were the basis for a religion, and many aspects of the stories were used to focus worshippers' attention, and they were therefore treated by many at the time as historical facts. They focused their attention on those gods and goddesses that were consistent with their beliefs and values.

The best example that I can use to demonstrate the challenge of chronology, is referencing a main character known as Pandora. As she is the first human woman, she features in her own story, but she was created by Hephaestus, the son of Zeus and Hera, and it happened when Zeus and Hera were already married. But Zeus met and fell in love with Europa, a human woman, who was alive before he married

Hera, and before he had a son to ask to make the first woman. Challenging!

As an author with a particular attention to detail, (at least I believe I do), the chronology of Greek mythological events became increasing important to me as the list of novellas planned for this series grew to thirteen.

I have therefore prepared a simple chronology (that may or may not be consistent with other writers of this genre) to assist readers in sorting out the sequence of events that occur in the stories that I am sharing with you. (Spoiler alert!)

I now believe that Greek Mythology Chronology should be a legitimised field of study all on its own. (Perhaps it already is?)

The novella.	The details of the event.
Pisces	Gaia forms the earth, oceans and skies. She is the earth mother.
Pisces	Gaia gives birth to Uranus.
Pisces	Cronus is born and defeats Uranus when he is released from confinement.
Pisces	Aphrodite is born.
Capricorn	Pricus is the father of the sea-goats.
Pisces	Cronus is crowned king and marries Rea. Zeus is one of their six children.
Centaurus	Cronus mates with Philyra. Chiron is born.
Pandora	Prometheus creates a race of human men - It is known as the golden age.
Pisces	Zeus defeats Cronus and Zeus is crowned King of the Gods.
Pisces	Zeus marries Metis, Athena is born, but Metis dies.

Pandora	Prometheus creates a second race of human men - It is known as the silver age.
Pandora	Prometheus creates a third race of human men - It is known as the bronze age.
Pisces	Zeus marries but then quickly divorces Themis.
Pandora	Prometheus creates a fourth race of human men - It is known as the iron age.
Sagittarius	Crotus invents the bow and arrow.
Pisces	Zeus marries Hera. Ares, Eileithyia, Hephaestus, and Hebe are born.
Pisces	Aphrodite arrives at Mount Olympus and marries Hephaestus.
Pandora	Hephaestus creates Pandora as the first human woman.
Taurus	Zeus meets Europa.
Scorpio	Zeus mates with Leto and Apollo and Artemis are born.
Scorpio	Poseidon mates with Euryale and Orion is born.
Scorpio	Atalanta is recused as an infant and she now runs with Artemis
Aries	Zeus creates a cloud nymph named Nephele.
Aries	Poseidon mates with Theophane and Chrysomallos is born.
Aries	Nephele marries Athamas and Helle and Phrixus are born.
Aries	Chrysomallos rescues Helle and Phrixus.
Ophiuchus	Apollo mates with Coronis and Asclepius is born.
Cancer/Leo	Zeus mates with Alkmene and Herakles is born.
Gemini	Zeus mates with Leda and Polydeuces and Castor are born.

Pisces	Aphrodite mates with Ares. Eros is born.
Scorpio	Orion meets and befriends Hephaistos.
Virgo/Libra	Zeus visits Themis and Astraea.
Cancer/Leo	Herakles is assigned the first of his ten labours.
Cancer/Leo	Herakles befriends Chiron.
Centaurus	Chiron befriends Herakles.
Gemini	Castor and Polydeuces join the Argo crew
Cancer/Leo	Herakles joins Argo crew.
Gemini	Atalanta asks to join Argo crew.
Scorpio	Orion meets Artemis.
Centaurus	Chiron commences as a teacher.
Gemini	Herakles is inadvertently separated from the Argo.
Cancer/Leo	Herakles resumes his labours.
Scorpio	Orion duels with the giant scorpion.
Gemini	Jason and Argo crew return with the Golden Fleece.
Gemini	Calydonian Boar Hunt.
Gemini	Atalanta joins the Calydonian Boar Hunt
Cancer/Leo	Herakles accidentally wounds Chiron
Centaurus	Chiron makes his plea to Zeus.
Pisces	The Greeks and the Trojans start a war that lasts ten years.
Aquarius	Zeus meets Ganymede.
Cancer/Leo	Herakles becomes immortal and marries Hebe.
Pisces	Atalanta competes in a running race against her potential suitors.
Gemini	Castor and Polydeuces become immortal.
Pisces	Aphrodite an Eros escape Typhon.

1

The constellation - Aries.

During Zeus' tempestuous marriage to his wife, Hera, he had many, not so discreet liaisons with both goddesses and human women alike. He had good taste, as they were all beautiful, nubile, and for the most part willing and appreciative of his sexual skill sets. Hera was typically jealous of all of them. She blamed the women who allowed themselves to become involved with her husband, despite knowing that as the supreme god, that they were essentially ensnared by his charm or his godly powers.

Sadly, for Hera, as the goddess of fidelity, among many other things, she was the subject of much humourous gossip by the other goddesses of Mount Olympians and by the humans who were supposed to worship her. Hera believed that her husband set a disappointing example, and his behaviour defied her beliefs and teachings. Hera understood that his behaviour diminished the much-needed respect that they both required for their position as King and Queen of all of the Gods, but Zeus didn't care. He said he did, but she knew he didn't.

She herself, showed no desire in having any affairs outside of her stormy marriage. She didn't contemplate revenge sex with another man, as she never had any desire to do so. In truth, she knew that Zeus wouldn't care if she did, so it was pointless contemplating doing it as it would have no effect on him. She often complained to him about his infidelities, and he always promised to be faithful, but they both knew that the truth of his words only meant that he'd try harder to be inconspicuous next time. He would endeavour to be more discreet when he was being sexually active with another female. That happened more often than she liked, but less often than what he desired.

Zeus' and Hera's sex life with each other was deemed satisfactory by both of them, though that was never openly spoken about. Hera knew that her husband's wandering lust was not as a result of her own inability to satisfy him. He never complained about their sexual frequency, and he was always delighted and responsive when she initiated sex between them. Their intimate sexual pleasures were fun and also reliably mutually satisfying.

Hera was a beautiful woman. She knew she had sex appeal and she noticed the appreciative and admiring stares that other males sometimes gave her. She didn't wear revealing clothing that specifically attracted attention. She would never knowingly titillate males with suggestive language or femininely charged sexually gestures. Her stance on fidelity remained her strong and well publicised commitment, even though there were many males who would readily accept an invitation to bed her.

Most of the time her suitors were discouraged by her lack of receptivity, and they graciously refrained from pursuing the idea of intimacy with her. However, there was one human man who became obsessed with her. His name was Ixion, and he was the King of the Lapiths. He was forever seeking her out for advice about his kingdom, on how to be a better king, and on how to rule his subjects with benevolence, and most importantly to him, on how to find true love.

At first, she took the task of counselling him seriously. She found him to be receptive to her advice and principles. He seemed eager to learn more, and he enthusiastically demonstrated that he was capable of understanding and implementing her advice. He had obviously benefited from her guidance.

Then, after several visits with her, he stepped up his amorous intentions toward her. He drew closer to her, moving into her personal space. He tried touching her, and he would lean forward to initiate a kiss between them. Initially, Hera was gracious and she gently dismissed his advances. She convinced herself that she wasn't troubled by them, but still, she decided she would stop seeing him. She instructed her staff to not take any more appointments from him. She hoped that he would get the message, and find someone more suitable and more receptive to his intimate needs.

She was wrong, her dismissal of him only excited Ixion. He believed it was her way of making him try harder to be with her, that he somehow needed to prove his commitment to be worthy of her affections. He started writing adoring letters to her, professing his admiration, respect, and then finally he offered her his undying love. He sent her several magnificent arrangements of flowers and sexually suggestive gifts, but she rejected all of them. After that, it became more serious, he raided his own kingdom's treasury to give her gifts of gold and jewellery.

Hera did not want this to escalate any further. She especially did not want Ixion's infatuation with her to become public knowledge. She began to dread the potential for public ridicule, and even worse, she feared Zeus' punishment for this man's behaviour when he eventually learned of it from others. So, she took the initiative and complained to her husband about the unwanted attentions that she received from Ixion. She easily convinced him that his advances were unwanted, and that the love he loudly professed was both disturbing to her and completely rejected.

Zeus took Hera's news well. He didn't admonish her for allowing this to manifest. He accepted that some males can be overly zealous in their pursuit of a desirable female. He knew that his wife was attractive, and so he wasn't surprised, or angry, or even upset that this had occurred. He wasn't even slightly jealous, and this disappointed Hera just a tiny bit, as it would have been satisfying if he had felt just slightly threatened by another suitor. Hera suspected that her husband may have even been moderately amused by her predicament.

Zeus agreed to assist Hera in discouraging Ixion from unwanted attentions, but only after a lengthy heated verbal exchange, that resulted in Zeus promising Hera that no harm would come to the man. She insisted on a resolution that preserved everyone's dignity.

Zeus gathered his staff. He instructed them to prepare a civic celebration of human progress for those who lived under the watchful guidance of the Gods and Goddesses of Mount Olympus. The occasion was to mark the future of greater collaboration, and a clearer understanding of current human challenges. They would meet to discuss human needs and how to assist them to be more independent, whilst maintaining a moral imperative to obey and worship their gods.

In truth, the whole event was a simple ruse to lure human nobles to the gathering, so that Ixion would feel receptive about being included on the honour role of notable special guests. In reality, Zeus didn't much care for the agenda, he just wanted Ixion to willingly attend and to be relaxed and off his guard. He wanted to observe Ixion's behaviour toward Hera first hand.

The guests arrived on the appointed day, all of them dressed in special event attire. They were babbling excitedly about the programme, and the opportunity to mingle with the elite of their Gods, and were especially excited about the prospect of independent prosperity of the elite people. Ixion was among the group of attendees, and he was just as delighted as the others to be included in the feastings and discussions. He was also delighted as it would give him another opportunity to be close to his beloved Hera. Maybe she had thought about him, and possibly her feelings were mellowing toward him. He savoured the moment when he could properly express his devotion to her.

Zeus had arranged for a beautiful cloud goddess named Nephele, a nymph, to transform herself into the exact copy of his wife, Hera. He ordered her to publicly mimic his wife's behaviour and to mingle with the humans, so that she could report back the nature of their utterings to him. Nephele, was only too happy to oblige and please her King. She did as she was asked in the belief that he was gaining insights that would help him maintain his edge during the proceedings. Zeus told her of Ixion's value at the gathering, and Nephele quickly understood that he was a priority. He also cautioned her that Ixion had developed an infatuation for Hera, and that she should do her best to gently dissuade him, should he make any disrespectable suggestions or advances.

Nephele never asked why Hera wasn't in attendance. Hera was often away from Mount Olympus. She just assumed she was busy attending to one of her many other duties.

Zeus' plan was to observe Ixion's actions when he believed he was with Hera, but was actually with Nephele. This was in order to safely test Ixion's true intentions without putting his own wife at risk.

The guests mingled, talked, planned, agreed, and disagreed on many things, as they drank wine. They feasted, talked louder, and they drank even more wine. Presenters presented and scribes scribbled. They laughed often, and towards the end of the evening, they congratulated each other on a brilliant event and the promise of a brighter future for everyone.

After the feast, an inebriated Ixion declared his lust to Hera, not realising he was addressing Nephele. As arranged, she calmly spurned him, but his lust for her overpowered his sensibility and he lost his self-control. In his drunken rage, he gathered her in an overpowering embrace and forced her into an adjoining empty guest room bed chamber. Before she could react, her skirts were thrown up over her hips and he was aggressively penetrating her. He violated and hurt her, all whilst professing his disappointment in her that she did not reciprocate the love and kindness that he offered her. He quickly spilled his seed. He looked embarrassed as she turned to face her rapist. He mumbled a feeble apology and turned and fled the room.

As Ixion fled the scene, Zeus had seen him urgently depart the palace. He became concerned for Nephele. When he found her lying on the bed, she looked disheveled and was openly weeping. She explained what happened and that she had been savagely raped by Ixion. She was taken completely by surprise, and she couldn't understand why she hadn't used her goddess powers to stop him. It all just happened so fast that she didn't have time to react. She was trying to be kind to him, but he had violated her.

Zeus summoned handmaids to assist her. He sat beside her and hugged her, professing his sorrow that this had happened. He promised her that Ixion would be found and punished for his crime.

***

There was no trial. There was no court hearing. There was no defence for Ixion's behaviour. No-one attempted to defend him. Zeus punished Ixion for raping Nephele and for his persistent lust for Hera. He arranged for Hermès to escort him to his brother Hades with the instructions that Ixion would be lashed to a fiery burning wheel with numerous venomous serpents to restrain him. If he struggled, the snakes would attack and their venom would render him in absolute agony.

The wheel, which would turn slowly for an eternity, was located deep within the bowels of the worst part of the Tartarus underworld. There, Ixion would only have the screams and nightmares of all the other tortured captives to keep him company. It was the worst kind of fate for a sexual predator, and beyond anything that anyone could have ever imagined.

News of Ixion's fate spread quickly throughout the human population, and for long-time humans were more compliant, obedient, and sincerely grateful toward their godly masters. And, for a short while, acts of sexual violence diminished. Perpetrators were warned.

Sadly, for Nephele, she discovered that she had been impregnated by Ixion. She was ably assisted throughout her accelerated pregnancy, but as the baby was conceived in violence, she sadly gave birth to a deformed son. She named him Ixionidae, and she tried her best to nurture and to love him. She endeavoured to raise him as best she could, but both his features and his soul were full of ugliness. His laughter was sinister. Even as a child, he assaulted human females menacingly, by publicly offering his exposed engorged penis to them, pressing on them to receive him and to have some wicked fun. He delighted at their screams and panic as they fled from him.

Ixionidae had grown up quickly and he was a worse sexual transgressor than his father. As he grew taller, he was confined to work in the stables, where he was forbidden to come close to any human females. His evil lust continued to manifest and so in his sexual frustration he violated a mare. The resultant birth was the first of the Centaurs, a half man, half horse creature. It was full of rage and it engaged in a frenzied attack on the mare that bore him, killing her with his hooves. Ixionidae watched the violence, laughing gleefully at the gore.

Nephele decided she would permanently leave Mount Olympus. She was afraid of Ixionidae and what he had become. Zeus hadn't offered her any real protection from her son, and she had felt that it was better for her to leave. She decided she would start a new life, far away from Mount Olympus and the shallow debauchery of the gods and goddesses. She aspired to find her place among the humans and hoped to lead a calm and peaceful life with them.

When Zeus learned of Nephele's sudden departure, he felt ashamed of his own behaviour and realised he should have done more for her. With Nephele departed, he banished Ixionidae from Mount Olympus. He, and his centaur son went to live on a mountain named Pelion, where they roamed the hills and plains, living a wild feral life. Ixionidae mated with many of the Magnesian mares, and they bore him many more Centaurs who were all aggressive savages like himself. He was their king, and as a herd, they terrorised the local population and any travelers that happened to come their way.

***

Nephele traveled alone and by foot. She was sometimes offered a seat on a cart or a carriage which she accepted when she was tired or felt the need for company. Being a cloud goddess, she could direct rain bearing clouds away from her so she never needed shelter from inclement weather. She packed light and carried her scant possessions in a bag that she had designed to carry on her back. The weight of her meagre possessions was evenly distributed, and she had made broad straps that fitted over her shoulders to comfortably carry the load. The backpack allowed her arms and hands the freedom to do other things whilst keeping her possessions safely with her. She earned food and shelter by amusing her temporary hosts and benefactors by shaping the clouds into images of animals and other recognisable objects. This delighted many and some queued to reward her so she would provide further amusement. Even today, when we humans gaze into the day-time skies, we sometimes see that the clouds have formed recognisable images as a legacy to the cloud goddess, Nephele.

Nephele was pleased that she was fondly regarded and generally well cared for wherever she visited, but she continued to travel until she came to the City of Orchomenus in Boeotia. Boeotia was a lovely and peaceful region, and it was there that she finally felt safe. She was polite, friendly, and amusing to the gentry of Boeotia.

With her powers over the shapes of clouds, she soon came to the attention of a merchant named, Erastus. He was especially intrigued by her luggage and asked her if he could examine it. She obliged in exchange for some hot food and a bed for the night. During the course of the meal, Erastus and his wife Esmeralda got to know Nephele and they were delighted with her company. When she hesitantly explained her troubled past, skipping the worst of the details, they were immediately sympathetic.

Erastus and Esmeralda glanced at each other and shared a knowing glance. Their imperceptible nods were used to communicate a plan of action. 'Nephele,' Erastus said to get her attention. He was smiling broadly and seemed pleased with himself.

Nephele had eaten well. She had had a glass of wine, but its normally intoxicating effect didn't have any influence on her. Gods and Goddesses could choose inebriation. She turned to face her host.

'Esmeralda and I are absolutely impressed with you,' Erastus explained.

She glanced at Esmeralda who smiled nodding her agreement.

'Thank you.' Now everyone was smiling.

'We'd like to offer you a position on our staff.'

Nephele didn't see herself being engaged as a cook or house keeper. She felt she had more to offer. She was sufficiently astute to simply nod her intrigue and encourage Erastus to continue.

'We'd like you to design a range of luggage that can be used by travellers. You obviously have skill with design and fabrication. Together, we'll supply the markets all over the country, and importantly, we'll share the profits. You will have room and board with us, we have plenty of spare rooms, you can design the packs that are carried comfortably on people's backs. You'll run the workshop, and we'll all share the spoils. What do you think?' he asked hopefully.

'I think that is an excellent idea,' Nephele replied and she looked genuinely pleased and happy with it.

'We can do them in a range of sizes and colours that will appeal to both men and women alike,' Esmeralda enthused.

'I have a few good ideas that I believe will work,' Nephele was on board. We can include holsters and pouches so that odd shaped items can be carried without interfering with delicate items packed within the pouch.'

'Fantastic,' Erastus was getting excited.

'And, I think we should call them, backpacks.'

'That's brilliant, Nephele. You are very clever,' Esmeralda proclaimed as she was just as much an entrepreneur as her husband, and she could immediately visualise the benefits of their collaboration.

***

Nephele busied herself with the designs of the backpacks. She ended up with three which were suitable for men and three that were suitable for women. Erastus got to work negotiating the fabrication of the cutting templates by a favoured blacksmith. They were made of polished rounded steel and when ready, the fabric was laid flat on the cutting table and the template rested on top. The worker carefully followed the outline of the steel with a sharpened cutter and the resultant cut section of fabric was the perfect shape for further assembly. The blacksmith was ecstatic with his commission, and he ensured a high standard of quality work. He added handles so that they could efficiently be lifted from the cutting tables. Erastus was concerned that the various sizes would get jumbled, so Nephele decided that each template would be numbered and coded in such a way that they were easy to identify. Much to the consternation of other merchants, Esmeralda managed to secure an entire shipment of bolts of all-weather fabrics that would be used to manufacture the backpacks.

After Erastus found and secured a fabrication workshop, Nephele interviewed and recruited the needlewomen needed to sew together the pre-cut fabrics into the six different styles. They started with three experienced women, paid them well, worked them hard, treated them with respect, and soon the finished backpacks were on display.

Fortunately, Erastus listened to Nephele's and Esmeralda's advice on their pricing policy. Originally, he wanted to sell them at a discounted price to attract interest. But the two women were firm and insisted on a higher price as these were new to the market and they had a head start on the competition. There would be a time for discounting, but only if needed later.

Erastus engaged some young people to demonstrate their use to potential customers as they passed by the retail store. Immediately on their release, they had sold two weeks' worth of production in a single day. The backpacks were a success.

The following day there was a queue of people waiting outside their shop to buy a backpack. Orders were taken, names recorded, deposits paid, and more cutters and needlewomen were engaged to help speed up production.

Erastus was delighted. Not only were the backpacks a huge success, but customers bought many other things from his retail store. Business was booming.

Esmeralda gave her husband a loving appreciative hug. She was pleased that he listened and had allowed himself to be guided by women who she maintained had much to contribute.

***

The local economy was generally thriving and the people were mostly contented. Their King was both intelligent and benevolent. He showed a keen interest in the day-to-day dealings of merchants, fabricators, engineers, farmers, and transport enterprises, that operated from within his kingdom. He contributed to infrastructure that encouraged investment, and his taxation policies were reasonable, and for the most part the monies raised were seen to be reinvested for the benefit of the community.

The king maintained a small standing army that kept a vigil against bandits, and generally kept law and order on the streets. The officers and soldiers were respected and obeyed and crimes were negligible. The bulk of the inhabitants of Orchomenus wanted to feel safe, raise their families, enjoy life, and their compassionate king did his part to ensure that this was possible.

Every few months the king invited a select cross section of businessmen and their wives to his palace. He established a community forum which encouraged discussions which brought about mutual benefits for the kingdom and its people. Invitations were keenly sought after as the king followed the discussions with meaningful resolutions, and the people who attended felt proud of their contributions.

He provided his guests with a celebratory feast, showcasing local foods and wines. Each time the king hosted the event, it got to be a little more special. Life was good in Orchomenus, with one exception. Their beloved king, whose name was Athamas, was lonely.

***

Athamas had over the years received numerous offers to marry princesses that were of age from neighbouring kingdoms. He even met with a few of them. They were all nice, but he didn't want nice, he wanted love. The other kings offered alliances, peace, and security, through the creation of mutually beneficial family bonds. But Athamas didn't believe in this process. He firmly believed that to only marry for profit, or security, robbed the institution of marriage of all of its grace and dignity. He wanted romance and happiness, and to marry a woman that had wanted and loved him. Someone that shared his values and love for the people that he ruled. The women that were presented to him as potential brides, would be obedient and subservient to him. He wanted a wife that would challenge his ideas, help him run the kingdom, care for the people, and be loving toward him. Athamas was both a romantic and a realist. To be a father to the right type of children, he needed the right type of woman to be their mother. He knew that he would recognise her when the opportunity presented itself. Though Athamas was a patient man, he knew that time was against him. As he neared his thirtieth birthday and by local custom; it would be seen as a terrible omen by his people if he hadn't fathered a child by the time he was thirty-five.

***

The palace representative was standing in the doorway of Erastus' establishment. His visit presented them no consternation, as their reasons for coming were numerous and rarely of a worry to Erastus and Esmeralda. He was examining the backpacks that were on display.

'Erastus,' he began to speak, but paused. He lifted the largest of the backpacks off the display and closely examined it.

Erastus immediately understood the opportunity. 'Would you like to try it on?' he invited.

The man was known as a person with some authority to make decisions that benefited his king. His name was Leonidas and he was known as a cunning negotiator, a fair law maker, and he was also a family man. His wife and children frequented their establishment.

Leonidas had influence in all aspects of the local administration, the palace guards, and the military. He was a man of influence, one who should be treated with respect, and regarded as a conduit in communications with the king.

Erastus indicated that Leonidas should turn around as he assisted the man place is arms through the straps. He turned Leonidas around and fussed over him ensuring that the straps sat comfortably on his shoulders.

'How many talents can it carry?' he asked casually.

'This one is rated for one hundred and fifty.' This was equivalent to about the weight of a four-week-old weaner piglet.

'Can it be made to carry more?'

'How much more?'

'Three hundred and fifty talents?'

'If the order for a custom backpack were sufficiently large enough, then of course, we would be delighted to manufacture them for the right customer.'

Leonidas stared at Erastus.

Erastus recognised the sign and so he ventured to explain. 'You see, we will need to manufacture new steel templates to accommodate the fabrication of the much larger design. The blacksmith is not cheap, but he does do quality work.'

Leonidas turned toward Erastus. His face betrayed nothing. Finally, he spoke. 'Put this on the palace account,' he said as he slung the backpack over his shoulder.

Erastus hid his grin and nodded. 'Is there anything else I can do for you?'

'The king extends a warm invitation to you and Esmeralda to the palace for a council of chambers discussion followed by a feast. Your wife may attend and observe the business side of the event.'

'May I be so bold as to beg an invitation for our new business partner? She is the creator of these backpacks and our chief designer.' Erastus like to sound expansive about their business.

Leonidas was intrigued. 'Perhaps that can be accommodated,' he speculated. 'Could I meet this woman first?'

'Nephele!' Erastus called toward the doorway to the production room. He headed toward the door yelling, 'There is someone here who wants to meet with you.'

Nephele entered the room and looked at Leonidas with interest.

'You're new,' he observed. She was wearing her working clothes; her hair was messed up and she had numerous strands of multiple-coloured loose fabric threads hanging from her arms and chest. He was smiling broadly at her and despite her attire, he was clearly impressed with Nephele's appearance. He took a deep breath. 'I'm confident that his majesty would favour meeting you, Nephele.' He examined her up and down as if to imagine her in finer clothing. He nodded his approval, but seemed concerned. Is there a husband or guardian to consider?' he asked Nephele and then turned to look at Erastus.

Erastus shook his head. He turned to Nephele to explain. 'This is Leonidas. He works for the king and he is most interested in our backpacks.'

Nephele smiled. She was instantly delighted at the prospect of a large palace commission. She smiled warmly at this influencer and stepped closer toward him. 'Can I assist your decision making in any-way,' she offered suggestively without making it sexual.

Leonidas and Erastus shared a look. 'Yes, bring her,' he instructed the merchant. He handed Erastus a parchment with the invitation details, turned and left with the backpack slung over his shoulder.

'Esmeralda!' he called out. She peered around the doorway opening. 'Please add one large male backpack to the palace accounts.'
Esmerelda smiled and nodded.

'And select your finest dress, and choose something special for Nephele to wear. We are visiting the palace for an important conference, followed by a banquet as special guests of the king.'

'Horray!' the women squealed with delight.

***

On the day that Erastus took Esmeralda and Nephele as his guests to the feast held at the palace by their king, he had to wait an eternity for them to get ready. The two women fussed over every detail about their hygiene, the dresses, shoes, make-up, jewellery, and especially their hair. Dressed in his best clothes, he paced the room searching for something to distract him while he waited. Despite feeling somewhat impatient with both of them, they still managed to arrive at the palace at the scheduled time.

King Athamas was greeting his guests as they arrived. He knew Erastus, but he had never met Esmeralda before. He had also heard about Nephele from Leonidas, but he only had a confused description of her. Was she the tall, beautiful, statuesque woman that Leonidas wanted her to be, or was she just a simple seamstress? He imagined a weak-eyed, gnarly, hunchbacked, old woman, with cuts and needle marks on her hands. As Erastus and the two women approached, he hoped the merchant would have sufficient etiquette to know how to introduce the two women to him.

'Your majesty,' Erastus effused as he bowed. 'Please allow me to introduce my beloved wife, Esmeralda.'

Esmeralda blushed as the king offered his hand in greeting as she performed an awkward bow of her head whilst trying to maintain eye contact.

'I gather that you are both the brains and the beauty in your mercantile empire?' Athamas asked sporting a teasing grin.

'Oh, your majesty,' Esmeralda looked down with embarrassment but then she noticed Erastus was grinning broadly as he accepted that the tease was to be taken as a compliment to both of them. She drew in a deep breath in relief, her concerns at Erastus' feeling's being injured were instantly abated.

'So, this captivating woman must be, Nephele?' the king asked hopefully, his face betraying his delight at seeing her. He held out his hand which she received and he gently drew her nearer to him.

'My reputation proceeds me,' she replied with a generous smile.

'Your reputation grows with each moment.'

'We'll join some of the others,' Erastus suggested. He turned to his wife who nodded and they left the two to their introductions.

Athamas and Nephele hadn't even noticed that they had left.

Now other guests queued patiently to give their respects to the king, but the man was now mesmerised by the woman he was talking to. The king's ushers quickly diverted the line and Leonidas stepped forward to meet guests on his king's behalf. Between pleasantries, he regarded Athamas and smiled. It was gratifying to see his king and good friend happily engaged in conversation with this beautiful woman. Athamas had been alone for too long and he deserved some romance in his life.

***

'Nephele, when did you arrive in Orchomenus?' Athamas asked.

'Some months ago,' she replied.

'But, where are you from?' he queried clearly curious.

She hesitated but replied cautiously, 'I'm originally from Mount Olympus, but I've traveled a great deal since I left there.'

'Mount Olympus!' he exclaimed. 'Did you get to meet any of the gods?' he asked mockingly.

'Yes, I did,' she laughed. 'But don't think too highly of them,' she warned. 'They're not all that godly.'

'But I'm impressed,' he declared. 'Did you perform any tasks for the gods? Were you a seam-stress for them? he inquired. 'I haven't heard any stories about a Nephele being at Mount Olympus.'

'Sort off,' she answered. Then she added boldly. 'Oh, I never worked with clothing before coming here. Besides, we only make backpacks, not garments.'

'I see,' he replied but his face portrayed confusion.

'They did bequeath me with one gift, however.'

'What is it?' he asked. 'Was it your brain power, business acumen, or your beauty?' he speculated out loud.

'Well, yes to all of those, but it's much more substantial than that.' She was now teasing him and the twinkle in her eye made him smile.

'Tell me!' he begged.

'Why don't I show you,' she volunteered. She headed for the balcony, beckoning him to follow her. 'What is your favourite animal?' she asked.

'My horse,' he replied.

'Tell me about him.'

'He is a mighty grey stallion, and he has carried me faithfully for many years.'

'A horse, no, a stallion it is.' She turned to the skies and drew up her arms. A curious crowd now gathered about the King and Nephele. They watched with curiosity as the clouds gathered and took the shape of a mighty powerful stallion. The white clouds grew darker into grey.

The king was amazed and the crowds cheered and Erastus rubbed his hands in sheer delightful anticipation.

Erastus had hoped that Nephele would enchant the king and hoped it would mean that they would be awarded numerous supply contracts and trading concessions. His plan was working and he and Esmeralda shared a knowing grin.

'Do one more!' a person in the crowd called out. Nephele again with her arms in the sky formed the clouds into a giant eagle. The crowd cheered and applauded as the eagle shaped cloud drifted toward the horse and gently settled on its back.

'How do you...?'

'I am a cloud goddess,' she explained.

'Of course you are. Your name, Nephele means cloud. I thought you were named after the clouds, but you are the clouds. So that makes you an immortal.'

She smiled generously at her appreciative audience. She turned to the sky and formed a flock of sheep from the clouds and raced them toward a fence. The sheep frolicked and then jumped over the fence and continued running.

The gathered spectators laughed and their applause was expressively appreciative. But the look in Athamas eyes was more significant. He was captivated by her and he quickly decided that Nephele should be wooed and seduced. She had quickly won his heart and the affections of his people. Athamas also thought that with a goddess such as this in his heart and household, that the other gods may also favour him. That would be good. He ensured that she spent the whole evening by his side.

The speeches now seemed less critical to Athamas, but he and his merchant development team completed their presentations and were applauded by the guests. Question time helped clarify specifics, but there was no dissention among his guests. The banquet filled his guests with quality foods and wine, and they all seemed happy. His staff politely ushered them out of the palace at a respectable hour. Only Nephele was encouraged to linger and so she stayed and continued to get to know Athamas better.

***

Their relationship quickly blossomed and Nephele and Athamas were soon engaged to be married. She was happy at last. Her man was a king and totally devoted to her. He was loving and kind and generous. Nothing was too much trouble. Together they walked the streets of Orchomenus and she delighted the people by forming shapes with the clouds as they called out requests to her. They laughed often and were now deeply in love and they were delighted to be together.

The people of Boeotia were also pleased. Harmony descended on the people as they worked the fields and crafted beautiful items for trade. They built houses and shops and monuments. They held festivals and parades and feasts. They laboured and were well rewarded. Erastus' business grew and he employed many people. He was now favoured among the nobles, so trade was good and he and Esmeralda prospered.

Within months, as the gods would allow it, Nephele had some exciting news. 'My king,' she said getting Athamas' attention as they lay in bed exhausted from their vigorous love making.

'Yes, my Queen,' he replied dreamily. 'I'm asleep on a cloud of love. Why do you drain me, and then try to engage me in talk?' The gleam in his eye's spoke of love, passion, and a hint of playfulness. She smiled as she embraced him in their bed. She reached down and played with his now limp member. 'I thought there may be some lust left in this bone yet, if properly motivated,' she explained as she was softly tugging at his member.

'Sleep, I need sleep,' he begged, smiling.

'But I do have important news,' she teased his mind as she fondled his phallus.

'What is your news, my love,' he inquired gently, her playfulness now arousing him once more.

'I am with child,' she told him and she straddled his body and took him inside her, reaching forward to kiss him before he could respond. Torn between exquisite pleasure and the desire to cry out with joy of learning of the child in her womb, he grew enormous inside her and moaned in pleasure as his seed filled her once more.

She smiled at him as he lay sweating in heated exhaustion.

'So, do you want to sleep now?' she asked coyly?

'I do need sleep, but I also want to hear more about our child,' he replied.

'Rest my husband. It'll take me some months to hatch these two. We have plenty of time to talk when you have rested.' she told him.

'Twins!' he exclaimed as he was now wide awake and sitting upright in bed. 'How do you know?' he seemed puzzled.

She smiled. 'I can feel two distinct heart-beats, my love. Your seed is strong, you sexy man.'

'Heart-beats,' he mumbled. Then he added more excitedly, 'Heart-beats! So, you are well advanced?'

'I would think the equivalent of three Selene cycles my lord,' she answered.

'But that would mean that the first time we...' his voice trailed off in the belief that she'd become pregnant on the first time they had made love. 'You are truly are a gift from the gods,' he told her. They snuggled closely in bed feeling safe and in love, feeling the joy of the new lives that they had created.

'As a goddess, my time of pregnancy is reduced from that of a human female. I will quickly grow a swollen belly.'

'And I will love you all the more for it,' he assured her.

Athamas understood that this news would please his people. They had genuinely taken to Nephele and she was a positive role model to others, and she greatly assisted farmers with her powers over the clouds. She would bring them rain when needed for the crops. Not too much, but just enough so that the harvest would be perfect. Whenever Nephele learned of a villager's misfortune, she would visit and comfort them. She always had kind words and solid, positive advice. She was sought after when she walked the streets of his kingdom, and he was pleased that she contributed so generously to the overall prosperity of Boeotia.

Their wedding was a joyous event. There were many guests, plenty of food, and wine, and much revelry. Dionysus was toasted on many occasions, but he wasn't present for the festivities. The only two gods that were invited to her wedding were two that she trusted to keep her happiness and her location from becoming the topic of gossip among the other immortals. They were her closest friends. Iris, goddess of the rainbow, and her consort, Zephyrus, the god of the west wind.

During the festivities, Nephele, Iris, and Zephyrus joined together to skillfully play with the clouds and rainbows in a delightful colourful display, much to the amusement of the guests.

Nephele gave the only speech of the evening. Apart from expressing her love and her commitment to Athamas and the people of Boeotia, she also warmly thanked Erastus and Esmeralda for their friendship and love. She publicly bequeathed them her share of their joint venture. She expressed her gratitude to the couple who had warmly welcomed her into their lives, and helped her meet this wonderful man that was now her husband.

Erastus and Esmeralda stood and bowed in gratitude.

Their celebration lasted long into the night, but Athamas and Nephele were able to sneak away to consummate their marriage, making sweet love for many hours. They hoped their guests would understand, and that they would be happy to entertain themselves.

***

Poseidon is best known as the supreme god of the seas and the oceans. He could manifest storms and monster waves. He was the middle brother to both Zeus and Hades. He and Zeus looked alike, and they behaved much in the same way doing the many things that they did. Whilst Zeus carried a thunderbolt, Poseidon was famous for carrying his trident. Unlike Hades, both Poseidon and Zeus were known for their numerous sexual conquests. One of his more interesting ones, was a discreet liaison he had with a stunningly beautiful female named Theophane.

Theophane was a nymph and also the granddaughter of Helios, the god of the sun. She glowed with beauty and was forever radiant.

Theophane had many suitors, but she was cautious and shy. She liked Poseidon a lot, and was excited by his powers, but she neither encouraged nor dissuaded his desire to have sex with her. Theophane knew that when Poseidon wanted someone, that he wouldn't desist until he succeeded. Male or female, Poseidon had his desires and his needs, and she knew that they would be satisfied.

In truth, Theophane enjoyed sex. She wasn't promiscuous like so many other nymphs she knew, but she did have desires, and she enjoyed the expectation of sex as much as the act itself. She didn't go on about it, like many males did, but when the opportunity arose, she was a willing participant, as long as he was kind and gentle. She knew that if handled correctly, Poseidon could be both. She also insisted that any acts of passion between them be totally discreet. She enjoyed a reputation of modesty and she insisted that Poseidon respect it. He believed that her simple demand would be rewarded with gratifying sex, so Poseidon, plagued with his desire to have her, readily capitulated.

Now, Poseidon didn't mind a bit of a challenge when persuading his lovers into his sexual embrace. He'd do the work in order to consummate his longings. As long as their requests were reasonable, and that they didn't take too long, he believed he was mostly accommodating. He did have a reputation to maintain after all. He wasn't going to be denied or told what he, God of the seas and oceans, could or couldn't do with his intended lover, but he also wanted them to enjoy the encounter for two reasons. Firstly, with quality came the potential for quantity. A repeat performance was highly desirable as less persuasion and preparation was required to achieve it. Secondly, any advancement in his reputation for pleasure increased other female's interest in him. As a bonus, any respect he earned as a lover would needle Zeus. Sexual conquests were a bit of an unspoken contest between them.

When the time came for Poseidon to take Theophane into his sexual embrace, she persuaded him to take them away from spying eyes. He agreed, and so they went to an island named Crissa, which was populated only with sheep. The shepherds visited infrequently as there was plenty of fresh water, lush grass, and a natural rocky overhang that provided shelter for the flock in inclement weather. There were no land predators as the shepherds had cleared the island of rats and wolves.

Poseidon gave Theophane a quick tour of the island and convinced her that here, they would be completely alone. He cheekily added that she could loudly express her pleasure of being made love to by a consummate lover of his skill and experience. Theophane smiled and nodded her willingness to proceed. She looked about, but could only see rocks and grass to lie on. They would be uncomfortable and she might get bruises. Poseidon was prepared. He led her to a place where he had prepared a bed made up of soft, clean, thick sheep skins, that he had fashioned for her. 'The air is cold,' she complained softly. So, Poseidon smiled and lit a fire with a pile of drift wood that he had gathered and prepared earlier. Soon the fire roared and she smiled as she was warm.

She slipped off her clothing and stood naked before him. Poseidon had enjoyed many lovers, but none had glowed so radiantly as Theophane, granddaughter to Helios, god of the sun. She was beautiful and she was perfectly proportioned. Her breasts were magnificent and her pubis was barely covered with hair. He became sexually excited and as his clothes fell, his member rose. Theophane lay back on the woolen bed and spread her legs wide apart to receive him. Their embrace was drawn out and mutually explosive. He was a god after all and he kept his promise not to disappoint her. She was uninhibited in vocalising the strength of her climaxes and this both pleased and excited Poseidon.

They rested. They drank wine and ate from the food hamper that Theophane had prepared for them. She knew that they would make love again and looked forward to it, happily. The next time would be less urgent, and she thought that she would take the lead and ride him until he once more exploded deep inside of her. She smiled and he smiled. She laughed at this and he laughed too.

'Why do you laugh my lord?' she asked him.

'I don't know,' he confessed. 'It made me happy to know that you are happy. It was funny the way you laughed, and so I laughed too.' They laughed again.

She hugged him and kissed him fully on the lips. Reaching down she felt him growing and she laughed again, skillfully playing with him with both hands as she teased his tongue with her own. She pushed him onto his back and was about to climb onto him and insert his member when they heard human noises. Her passion evaporated.

Poseidon was bewildered. He was stunned by the cessation of their passion. He was also confused by the sounds of humans on their island. Their cosy lover's nest was being invaded.

The shepherds had crossed the sea by boat when they had spotted smoke coming from the island. Concerned for the safety of their sheep, they immediately launched their boat and had sailed across to the island to put out the fire, and to check on the well-being of their flock.

'Damn,' exclaimed Poseidon. 'The smoke from our fire has attracted attention. They won't leave until they know the fire is out.'

'We'll be discovered,' she exclaimed, pulling on her clothes. 'We have to leave; we must go now!' she was becoming emphatic.

Poseidon indicated his enormous erection.' We can't leave with this, like this,' he told her.

'We can't do anything about that now,' she stammered, now becoming anxious. 'They will see us.'

Poseidon would not be moved. He would ejaculate first and then they would leave.

Inspiration hit her, 'Transform us into sheep and tup me,' she instructed him.

'What?' he asked, uncertain of where she was going with this?

'As sheep, it will appear natural for the ram to tup his ewe. Turn us into sheep and you can complete your deed.' she explained.

So, Poseidon, God of all the seas and the oceans, turned them into sheep. She turned her rear toward him and as the shepherds climbed the crest of the hillock that were protecting the lovers, Poseidon, now morphed into a mighty ram, mounted Theophane transformed into a ewe, and he was vigorously trying to spend his seed. This was much to the delight of the confused men who watched and wondered about the bed and the fire, at a place where their ram was pumping vigorously to increase the size of their flock.

The men searched about for a boat that might indicate visitors to the island, but they found nothing. They doused the fire and left the island.

***

Many months later, a largely pregnant Theophane returned to the island with Poseidon. Theophane decreed that their child would be born on the island of his conception. Poseidon had agreed. They had enjoyed numerous trysts during her pregnancy, and he was now feeling a special connectiveness with her. He had fathered many children and decided he would love this one as much as the others. That wasn't going to be much at all, as he had a reputation to protect after all. He was a god, wasn't he? And Theophane was a goddess. The children of gods were bound to have divine powers and so they tended not to need much of that parenting stuff that many fathers burdened themselves with.

Her contractions grew fierce and Theophane screamed in agony as she pushed a large baby boy with long, curly, golden hair into the world. She realised now that Poseidon would be ineffectual unless he was told what to do. 'Fetch me some warm water and pass me that blanket,' she yelled at him. She indicated a basket she had prepared and had brought with them. Poseidon didn't like being yelled at, but he quickly did what he was told. He was thinking that sex with this woman would no longer feature in his plans, when the baby cried. Then it brayed. Then it cried. The baby's parents were confused. The baby suddenly morphed into a lamb. The lamb's fleece was a rich golden colour. The lamb brayed at its parents and Theophane gathered it to her.

Poseidon appeared dumbstruck as to what to do or say. 'That's a bit of a surprise,' he ventured.

'You think giving birth to a Ram with Golden Fleece was completely unexpected?' she snapped at him. 'It must have happened when you came into me disguised as a ram.' She was thinking out aloud, trying to make sense of giving birth to a lamb. 'You know, when you tupped me,' she reminded him.

'That was your idea!' Poseidon defended himself.

'Only to weaken your erection,' she reminded him. 'You promised me that we would be alone on this island.'

'You were cold and wanted the fire,' he retorted. 'Why couldn't you have used your golden glow to keep warm? You are related to Helios after all. As granddaughter of the god of the sun, shouldn't you be able to keep warm all by yourself?' he accused.

'I wanted ambiance, I wanted to be seduced. I wanted to feel special,' she wailed. 'If I wanted a quickie, we wouldn't have had to come to this disgusting sheep infested island just for you to have your way with me!'

Poseidon said nothing.

'What do we do with this?' Theophane asked indicating the Golden Fleeced Ram that now slept in her arms.

'How would I know?' replied Poseidon defensively. 'You're its mother.'

The Ram morphed into a baby once more and hungrily sought out her breast. 'He's a thirsty little bugger,' Poseidon chided. 'I'll bet he'll be horny just like his father.'

Theophane squirmed.

They were both quiet for a moment.

'Do you think he'll want sex with girls or will he prefer sheep?' ventured Poseidon.

'What?' she looked at him, she was puzzled.

'When he is an adult, do you think he'll perform like a man or do it like a sheep?'

'Is that all you ever think about?' she asked him.

'No, of course not,' he defended. He then smiled, 'Especially not when I'm hungry.' He paused, 'But when he's older... I mean, it does make you wonder.'

Theophane said nothing.

'I hope he doesn't get the two confused,' he pondered.

'Might start a whole new trend,' she offered grinning. Shepherds can get lonely.

He laughed, but he then looked thoughtfully out toward the horizon. He was now wishing that he was somewhere else. It was as if the sea was calling him.

She continued to hold the baby to her breast and he fed noisily. 'This is weird,' she told him.

'Sure is,' he replied.

'No, I mean it's weird that he is already getting milk from me. Normally, it should take a day or so,' she explained.

'What is normal about giving birth to a baby boy that turns into a Ram with Golden Fleece?' Poseidon asked ironically.

'And on an island full of sheep,' she added.

'We are gods after all. Those normal human rules don't apply to us,' he told her.

'I suppose you are right,' she mused.

'What will we do with him?' he asked uncertainly.

'I'll raise him,' she replied. 'You won't have to do much, just visit us from time to time. I know you are always busy being God of the sea and all that,' she spoke with a hint of sarcasm.

'It's not easy being the god of the sea, you know. There are many demands on my time and everyone seems to need me for something...' his voice trailed off.

'Oh, you poor thing,' she teased. 'Please take us off this island. I'll teach this little fellow how to grow up as a human, and that he should only use his sheep form when absolutely necessary. Hopefully, he'll grow up to meet a nice girl and they'll do what comes naturally.' She winked at him and grinned.

'Now you're talking,' Poseidon was delighted and looked pleased. He felt relieved that Theophane was warming to the concept of raising such a unique child. He was especially glad that she had accepted that she would be doing so, without his continual presence.

The baby, now full of milk, burped contentedly. They laughed. The baby stretched out his arms and yawned. 'He is cute,' concluded his father. Theophane glowed brightly with a warm unexpected happiness. The baby began to transform once more in front of them and was once more a ram and he leapt out of her arms. From just above his front legs, he grew magnificent birdlike wings which he flapped vigorously, and rose into the air and was now flying above them in circles, braying as he flew.

'Well, isn't that something else altogether,' murmured Poseidon. 'Just when you think you've seen it all, this happens.'

'Your son, Pegasus is a flying horse. Why shouldn't you father a flying ram?'

'That's true,' he conceded.

'I'm going to be busy with this one,' she continued. She raised her hands up to the flying Ram with the Golden Fleece and he landed nearby and then gently climbed back into his mother's arms. The ram was now happily licking her face. Slowly, he morphed back into being a baby and was soon soundly asleep.

'What will we call him?' Poseidon asked.

'I shall name him, Chrysomallos, after his golden pelt.'

***

The years passed quickly for Nephele's and Athamas's twins. They were now in their mid-teens, well educated, gifted in music, and understood the nature of regal etiquette when pressed to do so. Their son, Phrixus, was being taught rudimentary hand to hand combat, basic leadership skills, and palace management. His numeracy and word skills also pleased his father, but he especially noted that he excelled in fighting techniques and strategy. He recognised in his son that he was a problem solver. Their daughter, Helle, was being taught cooking, child rearing, fashion, haberdashery, and grooming. She was annoyed with her father that Phrixus had the fun stuff to learn, while she was burdened with boring girly lessons. She had asked if she too could be taught how to physically defend herself, but her father's reaction to her request thwarted any future discussions on that topic.

Presently, the twins were chasing each other through the palace, as Phrixus was in hot pursuit of his annoying sister. She had just taken his sword, which was a recent gift from their father, and he was determined to get it back. But Helle had other plans. She often teased her brother. She loved him dearly, but sometimes the best way to get any attention from him was to torment him. When they were younger, she had seized his toys and pinched his favourite foods. She would tell fibs that would get him into a little trouble, but not too much so that he'd get punished. Phrixus had a temper and would get frustrated and chase her whilst shouting threats of recriminations. Helle laughed and her laughter slowed her pace. She knew he'd catch her and punish her, and that was part of the fun.

When they were younger there was little to tell the twins apart. In features they were extremely similar. Phrixus insisted that his hair be kept cut short and ensured that his sister would grow her hair long. This was supposed to stop comments about how cute they were as brother and sister, but it didn't. Phrixus was always determined to "build up his muscles." He was determined to become strong and respected.

'He looks just like a boy version of her,' some older woman had once declared, pointing at the twins in the market place. Phrixus immediately hated her for her verbal disrespect.

Now the differences between them were quite profound. Phrixus was now exceptionally strong and muscular. He had an olive complexion and a strong-featured face that could comfortably be described as handsome. His face was yet to achieve stubble, but he let the fluff grow in an attempt to appear older. He supported short dark brown hair that produced ringlets when it got too long. His father sometimes called him curly, which he didn't like, but he knew well enough to never complain as his father didn't abide whingeing children. Anyone's reference to his curls initiated an immediate shortening of hair length.

Helle had long curly dark brown hair and a softer olive complexion than her brother. Both brother and sister had light brown eyes, but there the similarities ended. Helle now sported a distinctive feminine face which was prone to endearing smiles. She was tall and a bit too much on the lean side according to their nanny, who seemed preoccupied with feeding them. Helle's breasts and womanly curves were already distinctive. She sometimes chose to dress as a boy, but to appear male her breasts needed binding, and as this process was uncomfortable, she rarely troubled herself to do so. It was obvious to her parents that Helle was going to be a beautiful woman, when she filled out a bit. Helle liked wearing boy's clothes, as they were quicker to put on, and more robust to manoeuvre in.

Their much younger brother, Makistos, was just a toddler and their mother spent a lot of her time with him. Sometimes, they would all sit together and Nephele would amuse them by forming funny cloud formations for them. Their father, Athamas was almost always busy being king and doing king things. They spent much of their time learning, and they made up games and amusements. They wore out their minders and tormented their tutors. Life was an amazing adventure for the twins, and they grew-up teasing each other, having fun, and having the freedom of the palace.

Nephele was aware that they would soon need to experience more of the outside world if they were to develop the adult skills required to function in modern society.

One day, when the twins were wrestling as they often did, Phrixus suddenly became aware that he was holding onto one of Helle's breasts. She examined his hand and then looked into his face. She wasn't angry, but she did seem surprised. He pulled his hand away, suddenly embarrassingly aware what he had done. Neither of the twins had much opportunity to meet other teenage boys and girls. They grew up together in close company, but this was the first time they paused their activities in a realisation that they were growing up, and that they had distinctive features that were anatomically different from each other.

'Did you enjoy yourself?' Helle teased her brother.

'I er. I've never felt one before,' Phrixus blushed.

'Please don't touch mine again,' Helle stated. There was no malice in her voice.

'Has anyone ever...' he hesitated. 'You know.' He motioned in appropriately.

'Touched my breasts?' Helle was alarmed at where he was heading with this topic of questioning.

'Yes.'

'No, of course not.'

'I've always wanted too. I mean, not yours, but with the girls I talk to in the village.'

'I'm sure one day you'll meet the right girl and she'll do a whole heap more than just let you grope her breasts.' Helle looked at him with mild disgust. Their mother had warned her of the male weakness for physical touching. She wasn't prepared to be touched by Phrixus, or any other boy, just yet. She believed that she would know when she was ready for that type of intimacy.

Phrixus nodded. He ached for that day. He had sometimes heard his parents doing it, and he often thought that would be the ultimate prize in his life, to one day being with a willing woman in that way.

***

Later that night, Phrixus lay alone in his bed. His erection needed serious attention and he knew how to achieve satisfying relief without making a tell-tale mess. He proceeded administering the required rhythm, but for some reason, this time it wasn't working. He started to think of how wonderful his sisters breast felt and he instantly gathered momentum. He then tried to remember the last time he had seen Helle naked, and suddenly the hot ejaculation burst from him.

Phrixus was troubled. He never imagined that he could think of his own sister in that way. Other women were fair game. Even his father had said as much. His words often rang in his head. "Have fun, explore your base desires with a willing, clean woman, who won't give you a sickness, a baby, or any trouble with another man."

Phrixus returned to his bed having carefully disposed of the mess. Before he knew what he was doing, he was playing with yet another erection, but this time he was imagining penetrating Helle. He now speculated about his sister and he wondered if she shared the same feelings for him. They had always been close and they happily shared everything. Would she now also share her body, with him. He wondered how she would react if he hinted to her that they should try doing it with each other. If she hesitated, he would say it was to gain experience, so that they would know what to do when the opportunity presented it-self to doing it with someone else. She wasn't angry with him when he reached out and cupped her breast with his hand and held onto it. She thought it innocent and was good about it. Maybe she enjoyed it as much as he did. Maybe she would want him in the same way he now desperately wanted her.

At least, he hoped she did.

***

Chrysomallos was now seventeen years old. He was handsome, fit, muscular, and tall for his age. His long hair was curly and golden, and when it caught the sun, it was as if it was on fire. His whole body glowed when he was happy in the same way that his mother's did.

He and his mother lived a quiet life. She had remained a single mother, preferring not to accept the offers of courtship from the local males. Chrysomallos was her only child and she loved him dearly.

Theophane had nurtured him and educated him the best she could. They had occasional visits from Poseidon, his father. Theophane and Poseidon had agreed that would be best for both of them. When gifts arrived of food, cloth, or coin, Theophane was neither grateful nor surprised. She didn't question them, and she utilised them quite automatically as it was her right as a mother of a child from Poseidon. Theophane was resourceful and she didn't need Poseidon's charity. But she wasn't so proud as to reject it either. She prided herself on being a practical and stoic person. Their home was remote, comfortable, secure from the elements and strangers, and they were able to farm enough food for themselves and still have a surplus for sale at the local markets.

They had friendly neighbours who were far enough away to give them privacy, but close enough to lend a helping hand when needed. They sometimes met socially, and Chrysomallos was generally on good terms with the neighbour's teenage children. Their daughter, who was only thirteen, had a bit of a crush on Chrysomallos, but he did his best to dissuade her. She was too young, not his type, and also, he was concerned about the potential for retribution from the parents and her brothers. He needn't have worried too much, as they all actively encouraged the girl's desires because they approved of Chrysomallos, and his kind and caring nature.

Life was good and they were all contented.

Chrysomallos, knew his father was the great 'god' Poseidon. He was matter of fact about it. During his father's brief and infrequent visits, he was neither delighted nor displeased to see him. Poseidon didn't fake at being overly paternal, and Chrysomallos didn't miss it, or need his father's affections.

There was never a pronouncement of Poseidon's visits. You couldn't plan or prepare for them. He would sometimes eat with them, but he never spent the night. His father and mother once had a physical relationship, but as far as Chrysomallos could tell, that wasn't happening between them anymore.

What Chrysomallos knew about sex mostly came from watching the farm animals doing it. He knew that human relationships were more complicated, but he understood the basics. He knew how he was conceived and he practiced morphing between is human and ram form daily. In his ram form, he felt no desire to tup an ewe. At all times, his proclivities were strictly human.

He loved flying, but his mother had taught him from when he was still only a toddler that he was never to be seen in the air by other people, as news of a flying golden fleeced ram would bring them too much unwanted attention. Chrysomallos understood and accepted this, and so he mostly flew very high, at night, or over the seas. He ritually checked for human observers before he morphed. His night vision was excellent as were his navigational skills.

In his human form, he liked to visit Orchomenus and mingle with people of his own age. He had talked to young women and fancied that they were attracted to him. Having long golden curly hair was a handsome feature, and he learned early to keep it clean and tidy so as to display it to its full advantage. If the other boys were jealous, they kept it to themselves. Chrysomallos was also tall and muscular, which tended to minimise the risk of being physically assaulted. He was astute enough to avoid girls that had boyfriends, and he liked it when the girls showed their interest in him by pursuing him for affection, so that he was clear on all the boundaries. He longed to consummate his sexual desires with one of them, one day.

At home he worked the gardens and tended to the livestock with his mother. He was skilled at home repairs, and he fashioned tools that benefited their tasks in the garden. Like his mother, he was resourceful and adaptive.

Poseidon arrived one morning and seemed interested in his son's wellbeing. 'What has he been up to?' he asked Theophane while looking at his son.

'He can answer for himself,' retorted Theophane.

'How are you, Chrysomallos?' Poseidon asked as he stepped closer to the boy.

'Good,' he replied.

'Humph,' Poseidon snorted. 'Can you give me more information than "good"'?

'I'm excellent, thank you father for asking about my well-being,' Chrysomallos ventured and smiled. He proudly added. 'I can now lift my own body weight.'

'That's good,' Poseidon ventured and he turned to Theophane. 'That is good, isn't it?'

'He's your son, you should have expected it,' Theophane replied curtly.

'Oh, of course,' Poseidon replied seemingly bewildered. 'How is your learning, your education?

'I can read, write, and count proficiently,' replied Chrysomallos. He wasn't boasting. 'And I can work out most maths problems in my head.'

'Can you still turn into a sheep?' he asked his son.

'Yes father.'

Poseidon winced.

Chrysomallos hid his smile. He didn't know if his reaction was because he called him father, or because he could do the change. 'And I can fly.'

'He only flies in the dark,' Theophane assured him. 'We don't want him to attract any unnecessary attention.'

'That's good.' Poseidon sat back in his chair. 'What about girls?' he asked.

'What about them?' Chrysomallos replied.

'Have you been with any?' he inquired.

'He's too young for that!' Theophane exclaimed.

'Nonsense,' said Poseidon. 'I'm sure that I was younger than he is now when I experienced my first.'

'I have friends, some of which are girls,' Chrysomallos emphasised, and then added 'I like spending time with girls as much as I do with the boys.'

'What about sheep?' his father asked.

'I don't talk to them, even though I can,' Chrysomallos explained. 'Sheep are boring. Its "hay this" or "grass that", or "follow me, but I don't know why, or where I'm going". I change into a flying ram only to have some fun. But I don't let my human friends see me do it, because they would freak out,' he explained with a knowing wink.

'So, you only do it at night-time,' concluded Poseidon.

'I'm good at flying in the dark,' Chrysomallos boasted.

'I see,' he replied flatly. Then he commanded, 'Show me.'

Chrysomallos glanced at Theophane who nodded her approval imperceptibly.

Chrysomallos dropped his clothing and morphed into a giant ram. His hair grew to cover his whole body turning into sheep's wool. His wool, or fleece, was vivid gold in colour, and he began to glow. Chrysomallos as the ram was huge. He was solidly built, and capable of comfortably carrying up to two adults on his back whilst flying. His horns grew outward from his skull and they twisted twice into loops above his head. The ram face turned to his father and spoke calmly and clearly. 'I'm learning how to control the glow so that I won't show up in the dark,' he explained.

Poseidon roared with laughter.

Chrysomallos exited the building and with mighty flaps of his wings, he rose up and flew into the sky.

Poseidon and Theophane had followed him outside and his father marvelled at the sight. He turned to Theophane and spoke calmly. 'He will be of age soon, so you must discuss his future options with him.'

'I believe he intends to one day choose a wife, and plans to live close to me to raise a family.'

'A worthy pursuit, but as a flying golden fleeced ram, he has enormous potential.'

'Too much so. Imagine what bounty would be paid to have a trophy such as a golden fleeced ram. Many an unscrupulous oppressor would love to have him stuffed, mounted, and displayed.

Poseidon said nothing and so Theophane took his silence as acceptance of what she believed to be true.

***

Princess Ino was now an adult of marrying age. She was the oldest of four daughters of the King of Thebes, and therefore technically she was heir to the throne. But as a woman, custom decreed that she could ascend, but that she wasn't allowed to rule. Their laws were such that she must marry a suitable man, and that he would rule in her place.

Her future husband would change his name to match her surname, and he rule the kingdom with all the rights and privileges, as if he had been born the eldest son of the king and his queen.

This troubled her father, Cadmus a great deal because Ino, his troublesome daughter, had on many occasions expressed her determination to only marry out of love, with no regard to her devotion to her father, or for the benefit of their kingdom. It wasn't that Ino was in love with anyone in particular. She remained aloof, and she seemed generally disinterested in men. Or, perhaps she was afraid that when she got introduced to someone that her father approved of, that he would commit her to marry, even though she might not like him. Love was a luxury and not in Cadmus's consideration.

The king was getting old. His daughters were also getting older, and they were starting to lose their youthful appeal. The longer it took them to reach a solution, the riskier the outcome. The king and queen feared a hasty matrimony and the wrong man succeeding him as king. He wanted time to train his successor in the ways of the people, and to become the type of king that would protect and nurture the people that he ruled. Cadmus wanted the handover to be trouble free and pleasing to his subjects. The next-in-line to the throne should be a man that the people respected and loved, and not one that ruled with fear tactics and brutal subjugation.

'Ino, your father and I are worried,' announced her mother, Harmonia.

Ino looked at her mother with anguish on her face. She knew this topic and had heard numerous monologues of it from her parents, teachers, and sisters, many times before. She and her mother were seated together on a couch. Ino sat still, but she dutifully maintained eye contact with her mother. Her objections to the process would be dismissed, so she had learned to say nothing and just let the lecture happen. Her silence was her response.

'You're not even trying!' Harmonia carried on, not expecting Ino to say anything. Ino always went quiet when she was being reprimanded. She seemed not to say much at all these days. 'There is little point trying to be rational with you, my girl.'

Ino managed to suppress a smile.

'Your father and I have assembled suitable men for you to meet,' Harmonia announced.

'But mother, they are vultures.' retorted Ino softly. 'They come to lust on me, and then they will pick the palace coffers clean.'

Harmonia turned and held onto Ino by her shoulders. 'That may be true. But these particular vultures are all rich, handsome, and suitably charming,' she explained to her.

'But Mother,' whinged Ino. 'They are all charming when they want something.'

'Please,' begged Harmonia. 'Meet with them, get to know them and then decide on one.' She paused to examine her daughter to get the measure of her resolve. 'One day, soon, you must agree to one of them becoming your husband.'

'I'll meet with them,' Ino capitulated. 'And I'll try to like at least one of them,' she added.

Her mother embraced her, but she did not feel the warmth of a mother's love, just her relief. Her mother departed and Ino stood inert. She felt lost, defeated, and especially sad.

She had heard it all from her parents so many times. 'Ino needs to marry.' and 'Love is a bonus,' and 'She needs a husband whom can father a worthy heir to the throne and keep our royal line alive.' She felt sick. All she was in this equation, was a vessel for producing babies. She didn't even know if she liked babies. She had detested being responsible for her younger sisters when they were small.

She was painfully aware that if she didn't willingly participate in the process, then she'd be excluded from it. Her "husband" would be selected for her. If he forcibly had sex with her and claimed it was done to produce a child, they would all look the other way. A husband cannot rape his wife and sex with him was mandatory. Maybe she'd get drunk, she mused, possibly to the point of being so inebriated as to dull the memory of what he was doing to her.

She silently walked into the main hall and quickly hid. From behind a curtain, she discreetly peeked around the fabric. She saw that there were five men seated in the room. They were all as her mother had described them, but presently, they were busy glaring at each other. They didn't speak, though she suspected that they all knew each other, at least by reputation. She thought they looked like frustrated stallions waiting to see which one of them would be selected to seed the mare. She was that mare. Would her father give her to sex before the wedding, she wondered. He wanted a grandson quite desperately. She hadn't thought of that possibility before.

All these men would promise her love and respect leading up to their wedding day. What she feared was their behaviour after the honeymoon period faded. He would be busy learning to be a king, at best he would have no time for her, and at worst he would grow to dislike her and avoid her.

Ino pondered her fate. She didn't like her prognosis.

So, instead of going to the throne room as commanded by her parents, she went to her own room. She took a traveling bag and packed into it some clothes, some gold coins, and her favourite perfume. She next changed into street clothes and put on sensible walking shoes.

Ino had decided to abdicate her role as the king's eldest daughter. One of her other sisters could become queen and she would marry for her family's sake. Why couldn't her mother have given birth to a male? That would have made succession so much easier for everyone.

She scaled down the wall from her window. Her window faced a private courtyard and offered her the privacy she needed as a princess. The descent was a feat that she had performed many times as a child and she now walked casually through the palace grounds, and calmly, she stepped through the palace gates. The guard was presently distracted with some attractive women, and so no one who knew her personally, had observed her departure.

She quietly blended into the crowds with plans to immediately leave the city.

***

Over the next few weeks, Ino walked inconspicuously through many villages. She managed to trade her gold coins for smaller denominations', and she used her money sparingly to purchase meals. To stretch out her slowly diminishing fortune, she slept rough under the stars. Fortunately for her, the grassy fields were clean and soft, and the nights were warm, and the breezes were gentle. She was determined to rejected the offers from men who were traveling on their own, or in groups, who were overly enthusiastic when they invited her to join them.

She preferred the company of families. She would explain to them that she was in search of her parents who became separated from her during a fierce storm. They were instantly sympathetic, kind, and remained unobtrusive. She was grateful for their gifts of food, and happily shared their fire, and she joined in on the irrelevant conversations that families often had. To her, they were a novelty. To them, she was a curiosity. If they detected her noble upbringing, they chose to remain discreet about it. She never stayed with any one family for more than two nights, as she was concerned that they would become too familiar with her, and start asking awkward questions in an attempt to try to get to know her better.

Ino eventually came to the city of Orchomenus in the region of Boeotia. She had heard good things about this place. The people prospered under a benevolent king. The crops were bountiful, and the climate was pleasant.

She bought food from a merchant. He counted the coins. 'You don't have enough,' he explained to her after he'd priced the items.

'I'm sorry. I'm hungry and got carried away,' she apologised.

'You can have the food,' he told her. 'Just pay me the coin.'

'That is all that I have,' she informed him miserably.

'Then perhaps you will have to work for food, or you can earn coin by doing some honest work,' he advised her. 'Unless,' he said examining her clothing, 'You have rich parents to provide for you?'

'I'm an orphan,' she lied.

'A husband, siblings?'

She looked downcast, but said nothing.

'Poor you,' he replied insincerely. 'What will you do?'

'Work for coin, I guess,' she speculated.

'Would you like to work on your back?' he asked her blandly. 'A woman with your beauty can earn much for doing very little. I know a woman that can employ you, an she'll teach....'

'No!' she exclaimed.

'I understand,' he told her. 'You are gorgeous, and there is always plenty of coin for a girl such as you, all for doing what comes natural to many...'

'I'll use my brains, not my body,' she told him.

'Sadly, there is more money in using your body. Can you read?' he asked her.

'Yes, I can! And I can write, and I can count and tally ...' she declared.

'What is your name?' he asked her.

'Ino,' she answered.

'Ino, I need a bookkeeper,' he informed her. 'We will pay you a fair wage, and if you're good at your work, prove to be honest and trustworthy, we will treat you with respect. Stay, learn, earn, and be rewarded appropriately for your bookkeeping efforts.'

'What kind of reward?' she asked dubiously.

'Nothing like that,' he explained. 'My wife doesn't allow it,' he added shrugging his shoulders, even though he didn't appear bothered.

'Then I'll accept,' she said relieved. 'When do I start?'

'Considering how hungry I believe you are; I think you had better start straight away. Come with me.' He threw her an apple as he walked toward the rear of his establishment.

In the months that followed, Ino earned the merchant's respect. She quickly learned his business and was soon properly maintaining his business records, and adding value to the way they ran things.

Although his wife was initially cautious about Ino, the two women soon got on exceptionally well. Esmeralda quickly realised that Ino would become a valuable contributor to their business and she encouraged her by teaching her what she needed to know. The other workers accepted that hers was a senior position and they soon were taking their directions from her. Erastus and Esmeralda were growing to wholeheartedly like and appreciate this young woman, despite the fact that she insisted on being that person with no past, and no family.

***

Athamas declared there would be a feast to celebrate the twins sixteenth birthday. Nephele was pleased that her gentle suggestions had penetrated the mind of her busy husband.

Intimacy had waned between them over the past few years. She was willing, but it seemed that she wasn't in much demand. It didn't bother Nephele all that much, and it didn't seem to concern her husband. He busied himself with the affairs of state and keeping the kingdom wealthy. All he ever talked about in any detail with her was the weather, and that was only to remind her of where and when they needed rain.

She tried in vain to keep them close as a family and she consoled herself in the knowledge that at least she was there for their three children.

She had worked on the celebration idea for several weeks. Plans came easily into fruition when they were Athamas' ideas. She had to plant the suggestion in his mind. Naturally, he concluded that the feast would be a celebration of the prosperity of the family, the kingdom, as well as a birthday celebration for the twins.

Erastus was summoned to make arrangements for the provisions required. Nephele did not concern herself with these details. Her husband was an expert at arranging functions as well as being a powerful business person. Besides, he had numerous qualified staff to assist him.

Athamas had several rooms for his personal use from where he managed his kingdom. The larger room was where he met people with who he did business. He also had several smaller meeting rooms for confidential discussions, and a private den for when he preferred to work alone.

His office staff was educated, loyal, and hard working. They loved and protected him. Athamas knew how to reward their efforts with both praise and coin, and he and his team functioned well.

'My lord,' Pedro interrupted his master in his inner office.

Athamas looked up. 'Yes,' he answered.

'The merchant Erastus has been summoned, but it transpires that he has taken leave from his business, and he is currently holidaying on the coast with his wife,' Pedro explained.

'Oh, is that right?' replied Athamas. He had never imagined a person like Erastus being able to take a holiday.

'His bookkeeper has requested an audience to represent the merchant's interests. The bookkeeper wishes to know how best to serve you, my lord,' Perdo explained.

'A bookkeeper?' he responded. 'I didn't know he had a bookkeeper.'

'Shall I show her in?' Pedro asked.

'Her?' he asked in surprise. 'Yes, I suppose you had better. Bring her to the main room.'

'My lord.' Pedro did his customary small bow and retreated from the room.

By the time Athamas had entered the main office room, Ino was already waiting for him. She looked down at the floor as a mark of respect and submission.

'Show me your face,' he asked her and she showed herself to him. 'You are stunningly beautiful for a bookkeeper,' he informed her.

'Thank you, my lord,' she replied and inwardly smiled. She had managed to restrain herself from challenging his knowledge of the looks of bookkeepers.

'What do you know of provisioning my household? he asked.

'I have researched what your household has requested for previous events and I believe I know enough to arrange what you require. We'll have these supplies ready to deliver to you in good order,' she assured him.

'How long have you been working for Erastus?' he demanded.

'Nine weeks, my lord,' she replied.

'Nine weeks!' exclaimed Athamas. 'And you have researched my past transactions to calculate what we might need for an event, and you've done this even before I have started placing my order.' Athamas sounded impressed.

Ino said nothing.

'And Erastus trusts you enough to venture out on a holiday, and leave you in charge.'

'The trip is mostly a buying expedition. The holiday part was Esmeralda's idea.'

Athamas burst out in laughter.

Ino smiled. She was pleased that the king was in a good mood.

'If you are truly that good, I may need to poach you for my own staff,' he teased her.

'I would be honoured,' she responded, but hoped he wouldn't appoint her into his service.

Athamas studied her. She was truly beautiful, and if she was as smart as she claimed to be, then she could be useful in many ways.

Athamas found that his mind was wandering and that he was now trying to imagine being sexually physical with her. It had been quite some time since he and Nephele had been intimate. He knew deep down that it was as much his own fault as hers. Sadly, for both of them he had grown bored with her, so he threw himself into his work, and generally avoided dealing with their failing relationship. He studied the woman before him. If only he could have this woman to relieve some of his tension, he speculated to himself. He stopped thinking it abruptly.

She had stood there waiting for him to say something, acutely aware that he had been staring at her. She was uncomfortable and feeling vulnerable, but she remained still out of respect, becoming increasingly uncertain of what to say or do.

'Well,' he finally spoke. 'To business.' He gestured a seat at the table. 'My staff have prepared a list of items we require and when we need them.' He handed her the documents which she accepted and began to examine.

She worked through the document, making notes and asking the occasional question to gain clarification.

After quite some time working together, she finally said, 'We can have all of this delivered to you by the required date.'

'With my usual discount?' he asked.

'Of course, my lord,' she replied efficiently.

'Good,' he concluded. She was truly beautiful he thought. If only... his thoughts trailed off.

Then, almost urgently, he added. 'There is one other service I want you to perform for me.'

'Yes, my lord,' she replied enquiringly, unsure of where this was going.

'Tell me. Do you provide some comfort for your master?' he asked her.

'My lord?'

'Do you give him pleasure?'

'My work pleases him...'

'Are you intimate with him?' he spelled it out.

'No, my lord!' she burst out in surprise. 'I don't...' she spluttered. 'Besides, he's married and I know he doesn't expect that sort of thing from me.'

'I believe that I do. I do want you in that way,' explained Athamas, as a matter of fact. 'I hope you'll give yourself willingly to me. And, let me remind you that I am your king.'

He stood up before her and she looked up at him in total disbelief of what he was saying.

She was suddenly frightened. He was a king and had power over the life and death of all his subjects. Even though she wasn't from this kingdom, it would now be too difficult to explain her origins and furthermore, he wouldn't be interested in knowing. She was a princess and he had no right to violate her, but he would probably laugh if she tried explaining who she was, as if she was inventing some fantasy so that it would dissuade him. Her heart raced. She next thought to explain to him that she was a virgin. She would plead and get his understanding about her need to remain pure. Then she realised that by her being a virgin, that it might excite him even more knowing that she was unsullied and that he would be her first. She remembered her mother explaining to her, that if she calmly submitted, then she would have to endure less pain and injury. Her humiliation was another matter. She looked at him, her teary face betraying her reluctance to acquiesce. Finally, she felt completely trapped and left with no other option but to accommodate him.

'When?'

'Now will be appropriate. We won't be disturbed.'

'I...' she looked about the room searching for an escape.

'I won't hurt you,' he assured her.

He truly had no idea how much he already had.

'It would be best for your master's business if you could spare me an additional moment of your time and submit to me,' he added, now sounding supremely confident. It clearly excited him to be in full control of her.

Now her master's business, and with it her livelihood, was at stake. She had a difficult choice. Submit or lose everything, possibly even her life.

It seemed an age since he spoke. Her mind was racing.

'I'd be honoured, my lord,' she capitulated and hesitatingly moved toward him. Well, Ino thought, there has to be a first time for everything. She knew what to do as her mother had been candid about what she should expect when it happened to her.

'Not here,' he explained. 'We'll go into my private office.' He took her by the hand and led her to the smaller room. He shut the door and proceeded to open up his garments. He was already aroused.

With a large degree of uncertainty and hesitation, Ino bent forward before the king. She lifted up her skirts and revealed her sex to him. She felt him finger her, and she winced as the thrust of his manhood pushed deep inside of her. Athamas groaned in a whimper of pleasure and ejaculated just as the door opened and Nephele walked in on them.

'Athamas…' she started but stopped when she saw Ino bending forward before in front of her husband with is shaft pushed deep inside of her. Ino pulled forward, dropped her skirts and was now staring up at Nephele. His erection was rapidly losing its rigidity and he hastily pulled up is trousers and fastened them.

Nephele glared at both of them.

'I can explain,' assured Athamas knowing full well that he couldn't.

Ino turned and made to leave the room.

'Wait!' called Athamas.

She turned to face him. 'Yes, my lord? Will there be anything else?'

'Err, no. You may go,' he replied.

He turned to Nephele. 'I'm sorry, Nephele,' he apologised. 'I've been under much stress of late and we haven't been...' he tried to explain himself.

'That is your choice, Athamas. I have always been there for you. I'm a ready, willing, and devoted wife. Sex between us has always been lovely and mutually pleasurable. You had no need to violate that woman.'

'I know. I'm sorry for what I just did.' he explained sounding genuinely sorry for his actions.

'I am going to leave the palace for a while. I need time to think this through, Athamas,' she informed him.

'But the party... the twins... they will need their mother,' he countered.

'I'll try to return in time for that,' she assured him. 'You have completely betrayed the trust and love we once had, Athamas.'

'It was the first and last time,' he defended weakly.

'I'll bet...' she started to say. She now wanted desperately to accuse him of previous infidelities, but as she had no proof, she thought it best not to give him an opportunity for rebuttal. She drew in a deep breath and slowly exhaled, calmly walked near to him and spoke in gentle tones of admonishment. 'When it has been done once, we both know that it can happen again. Once that door has been opened, it can never be shut,' she concluded.

Nephele turned and hastily left his office. She stormed up to her private rooms, packed a travel bag, and then she explained what she was doing to her children, and their minders. She explained that she was going away for a short while. Their father would care for them, and she promised them that she would be back in time for their birthday party.

They both cried and held onto their mother, begging her not to leave them. She kissed them both, stood, turned, and calmly walked out of the room.

Within an hour she had left the city walls and was traveling on the back of a wagon. She was crying and sobbing. Her benevolent hosts knew who she was and were discreet enough to offer some comfort, transport, and to leave her to her sorrow. Behind them dark thunderous clouds began to form over the city. The people of Orchomenus were in for a long night of frighteningly fierce weather.

***

Ino had fled the palace in panic and confusion. She could never have imagined that she would have ever fallen victim to such a situation. She was angry, emotionally hurt, disgusted, and revolted by the king's behaviour.

She rushed into her personal quarters at the merchant's premises and bathed herself thoroughly. The image of his penis wouldn't leave her mind. How could he do such a thing? Were all men like that? Did their urges control them so much that they could so blatantly violate women as well as disgrace themselves. All to just forcibly push his man parts inside of a vulnerable woman's body. Was that a normal thing to do, or was she just naive? Wouldn't her body be more pleasing to a man during a genuine act of love-making. Wasn't he concerned he'd make a baby, or contract a disease?

She hoped that when he explained to his angry wife that this was the first time that he had ever done this with her. She didn't want any recriminations from the queen. If he was a sexual predator, then she now may become sick with some type of sexual affliction. She hoped she wasn't pregnant but she knew her cycle, and believed she was safe.

For the next few hours, she struggled with the questions that consumed her. Was it fear and loathing and contempt that she felt, or was it something else completely? She knew of women who controlled their men through the promises of sexual favour. She had vowed to never to become one of them. Maybe she was naive.

Ino then came to realise the deteriorating weather conditions outside. The lightning and thunder were disturbingly fierce, more so than she had ever experienced. The clouds were so dark that the day seemed to turn into night. The wind was howling fiercely and windows and doors rattled urgently.

There was urgent banging on the outside door. Ino went downstairs to investigate. She opened the peep door and saw that it was Erastus and Esmeralda. She pulled open the after-hours door bolts and they burst in the room just in time to escape the rapidly approaching torrential rain. Erastus slammed the door shut behind them and quickly secured the bolts

They were both panting from their haste, and shivering from the cold, and so Ino gathered blankets and did her best to comfort them.

'This storm!' exclaimed Erastus, 'It came out of nowhere.'

'I had only just become aware of it,' she explained. 'Then, I heard your banging on the door.'

'I'm so glad you were home and able to let us in,' said Esmeralda shivering.

'I thought you were still holidaying on the coast?' Ino inquired.

'We were,' replied Esmeralda caustically. She looked disappointed. 'But my husband "the entrepreneur" cannot leave his businesses for too long, and besides he was worried for you and the order from the palace, so he decided we would come home early.'

'As well we did,' declared Erastus. 'To be in this,' indicating the storm, 'at the coast could have been devastating for us.'

Ino told them 'Well, you are now both safe in your home. The building is shut tight and secure. There is nothing to worry about.'

'How was your visit to the palace?' asked Erastus.

'It was devastating to me,' she told them. She blushed, looked downcast and embarrassed.

'What? Why?' they both demanded.

Ino went on to tell them what had happened. She didn't spare any of the details. She was comforted that they had more concern for her, than for the order for the king's banquet. When she finished with Nephele's discovery of them, she showed them the order from the palace.

Erastus put the order aside. 'We have plenty of time to concern ourselves with that later,' he assured her. 'What are you going to do about the king?'

'That's easy,' advised Esmeralda. 'She has no need to ever go back there. She will remain safe here with us, and she will continue to do the bookkeeping. You will do the wheeling and dealing with the palace. Make sure that he knows that you know what he did to her. We can use it to maintain an advantage over him.'

'But,' protested Erastus, 'he violated Ino and betrayed Nephele. He must be brought to account.'

'He is the king. He will claim that he can do whatever he likes. The king is always above the law, because he is the law.

Ino was now forlorn.

***

Two days later Nephele arrived at an isolated house situated on the coast. It was far enough away from Boeotia for her to feel at peace. She didn't want to travel much farther for the sake of her children. She knew she'd return soon, and the more distance she traveled, the longer it would take for her to get back to them.

Over the two days on the road, she had enough time to think things through. She had decided that their marriage, as it was, was over. Perhaps she shouldn't have been surprised or angry at her husband's behaviour. Many men were victims of their own lust and depravity. She decided she couldn't forgive it, and that she would use it as a reason to move on with her life.

She was concerned for her children. They would be safe at the palace for now, and she'd figure a way to be with them soon.

Nephele now examined the house. Smoke drifted lazily from a chimney. She smelt food cooking and decided she was hungry, tired, and she felt brave enough to ask for food and shelter.

Her knock on the door was answered by a handsome young man with magnificent golden hair. He was tall and shapely and just old enough to support a whispery beard.

'Hello,' he said to her. 'What do you want? he asked.

'Kind sir,' she started to explain, but paused when he laughed. 'Why do you laugh?' she asked.

'I have never been called "sir" before,' he explained.

A woman came to the door and stood beside him. She also radiated warmth and had golden hair. Nephele concluded that they were mother and son. She spoke kindly but guardedly. 'Who are you?' she asked as she examined Nephele.

'My name is Nephele,' she answered. I am from Orchomenus and I have been travelling for the last two days,'

'You look exhausted,' added Theophane.

'I am exhausted,' agreed Nephele. 'May I come in? I can pay for food and shelter, if you'd would be so kind to invite me into your home,' she asked hopefully.

'Yes, come in,' invited Theophane. She motioned her son, Chrysomallos to step aside.

Nephele entered their modest home and looked about her. There were no surprises and little in the way of luxury or comfort. The fire glowed in its hearth, and Nephele was immediately drawn to the flames for warmth and comfort. 'Isn't it funny how a fire can evoke feeling of safety and warmth as well as being dangerous when left uncontrolled? Fire has such a godlike quality.'

'Do you know much about the gods?' Theophane asked her.

'I was originally from Mount Olympus,' she explained.

'Nephele is a cloud goddess Theophane explained to Chrysomallos. 'She is also the Queen.'

'You know of me?' Nephele exclaimed in surprise.

'We do.' And then added, 'I am Theophane, and this,' indicating Chrysomallos, 'is my handsome son, Chrysomallos.'

As they stood before her, she was attracted to their golden hair. Nephele searched her memory. 'You are the granddaughter of Helios,' she stated. 'No wonder you have golden hair. You do stand out with it.'

'Yes,' laughed Theophane. 'Greeks are famous for jet black hair. We do standout.'

'Your hair is beautiful', murmured Nephele, 'Are you married?'

'No,' she answered.

'You must get many suitors?' asked Nephele.

'The odd fellow shows interest. The thought of dealing with Poseidon drives them away quite quickly. Poseidon is Chrysomallos' father,' she explained.

'Oh,' said Nephele with understanding.

'We don't see much of him,' ventured Chrysomallos.

'Which suits us just fine,' added Theophane.

'May I stay awhile?' Nephele asked them.

'Yes, of course. Please be seated. Why did you leave Orchomenus? Theophane asked.

Nephele relaxed on a chair and Chrysomallos handed her a cup of water. She went on to explain about her life in Boeotia with her husband the king and their three children. She talked of her stress and loneliness, despite being married. She next described the scene when she walked in on her husband and that woman. The feelings of hurt and betrayal poured out of her. They were both good listeners. They were politely quiet when she paused, and were quick to offer her some more water when she appeared thirsty.

Theophane and Chrysomallos then talked a bit about their lives and Nephele found herself being interested in them. Their simple life with uncomplicated routines seemed attractive to her. They all seemed pleased that their conversation flowed so freely and natural.

Chrysomallos was curious about her children. Nephele described all three, but she noticed that Chrysomallos' interest peeked when she described her teenage daughter, Helle. Chrysomallos was a charming affable young man and she now hoped that the two would one day meet.

Nephele suddenly felt safe and welcomed by this mother and her son. She hoped that they would allow her to stay a while. Inwardly she began to relax and she realised that she had been burdened with considerable tension.

Theophane thought that she could easily become friends with this woman, and decided that if she wanted it, that she would help her.

Chrysomallos was eager to learn more about what a cloud goddess could do. He was too polite to ask before, but he would do so in the morning. He also wondered if the daughter of a cloud goddess had powers also. He imagined that she would be beautiful like her mother and he now hoped he would meet her one day.

As the day drew to a close, they set the table and sat to enjoy a cooked meal together. Nephele again expressed her gratitude at being welcomed in their home. 'This meal is perfect,' she said graciously.

After sharing their meal with her, they showed her a modest room that had a single bed and a few other items of simple furniture. 'The bed is comfortable, and you are welcome to use this room for as long as you would like it,' Theophane explained.

Nephele wept with relief. The two women hugged in solidarity. They were two goddesses that had been wronged by the men in their lives. They were both devoted mothers and they both experienced the agony of living in a harsh and unfair world.

Chrysomallos grew tired and informed them both that he was going to bed. He kissed is mother and then also kissed Nephele on the cheek in a familiar loving fashion. Nephele felt special that she had been welcomed so warmly into their home. It was only their first night together, and they already felt familiar and comfortable with each other.

It was after Chrysomallos went to bed that Nephele told Theophane about her experience at Mount Olympus. About how Zeus had used her as bait to trap a sexual predator and the crimes he perpetrated on her before he was caught and punished. She talked about her first son and how he grown into being a sexual monster.

Theophane listened and she sensed that Nephele had stored her anguishes for a long time. She was comfortable to hearing her story, but at the same time saddened by the details of the events that brought her to her door.

Nephele dried her eyes and looked at Theophane. 'I'm sorry. I have been unloading onto you. I would like to know more about you and Chrysomallos.'

'Well, our lives are simple, compared to yours,' Theophane concluded.

'You told me that Poseidon is Chrysomallos father. Were you close?'

'Less so, since he fathered my baby. I knew we wouldn't see much of each other. He is married to Amphitrite, and he has so many sexual partners that I knew that I was only being used as one of them. I don't resent him for it as I knew what he was like and I accepted it at the time. The sex with Poseidon, well let me assure you that it was amazing. But sadly, for me, I've never been with anyone since.'

'Does he visit?'

Not often and not for long. You see, Chrysomallos has a special talent and that keeps Poseidon interested in us. Without that, I believe we would never see him at all.'

'I'm intrigued.

'I'll let Chrysomallos decide if he wants you to know.'

The two women continued talking late into the night. They seemed comfortable sharing every intimate detail with each other, they felt a close bond and a relief that they could share their stories, the same way that loving caring sisters helped each other. Eventually, both women retired to their beds and slept.

***

Many weeks later, as the friendship between Nephele and Theophane and her son blossomed, the King of Boeotia was getting impatient.

'Where is she!' he demanded of Phrixus and Helle.

'We don't know,' replied Phrixus answering for both of them. Helle always went quiet when her father was in a rage, and even Phrixus was becoming concerned. Their father could be most unreasonable and they all depended on their mother to keep the peace and keep the family calm.

'We will have to continue to delay your celebrations until she returns,' he announced.

'Yes father,' he responded.

'Let me know if you hear of anything.'

'Yes father.'

Athamas hastily left the room. Despite being their father, he had always felt that they were her children. He had a kingdom to manage and left their upbringing to their mother. It was usual for a man in his position to do this. He was important and had responsibilities for the whole community. He believed that he would take a greater interest in his children as they got older and when they could take on adult responsibilities.

His plan was that Phrixus would one day be on the throne as his successor. When the time was right, he would commence teaching him. Helle would be married off to some worthy nobleman's son, and that would work to ensure the kingdoms continued prosperity.

Now his plans all seemed to depend on Nephele's return.

***

For a long time, intense feelings of guilt plagued Athamas. He felt foolish being caught in the act of obtaining stress relief through sex with a willing subject. She was accessible and his manly needs momentarily suppressed his normal high standard of fidelity. He was a king with regal powers and royal needs, but he was also just a man with needs also. He felt weak for succumbing to those urges with a woman other than his wife. He knew deep down that she would accommodate him if he expressed his desire to have coitus.

Athamas reasoning about his feelings soon progressed to self-justification. The problem with sex with Nephele was that it was predictable. Sex was boring. They would go through their routine motions and at the end of it, he would feel a brief elation. He would politely express his gratitude, and then go back to his normal activities. For a short while he'd feel good, but the memory of his brief moment of intimacy with her always quickly faded. If his wife gained any pleasure from their congress, she kept it to herself, as she wasn't the vigorous passionate lover of their earlier years. She used to express her pleasure vocally to the point where the whole palace knew what they were doing. He took it as a compliment, he wanted them to know and he prided himself on his sexual performance. Nowadays, he was certain the palace staff believed they were platonic.

Athamas thoughts advanced the belief that he was now experiencing a reawakening of his soul. Sex with Ino reinvigorated the proud sexual being that still lived inside of him. She had propelled him into sexual rapture, enlivened him, made him feel sexually adventurous once more. He was a king after all, and these feelings of empowerment over all others were his by proclamation. He had every right to fulfill his needs, where and when he needed them. He decided that he especially had the right to do so with whomever he chose. They were his subjects and therefore subjected to his needs. It was their honour bound duty to ensure his happiness and well-being. He was their ruler and they could not be happy, unless he was truly happy.

He now realised that Nephele was old news, his time with her was expended. Perhaps he was only at fault for taking so long to realise these problems. When Ino presented herself to him, it triggered a wave of clarity, and in that moment, he knew that he had to move away from the old and embark on a new adventure toward his destiny. The future was one of his favourite topics. He always talked the coming times with his advisors and with his subjects. Firstly, it distracted from the hardships of the present, but more significantly it gave them hope to believe that all the tomorrow's would be better.

Ino now represented his prospects for happiness. He would express his desire for her and she would be grateful, and fall in love with him, and they'll become married. He now had a plan. He would publicly annul his marriage to Nephele due to her abandonment of their marital bed. He would question her continued unexplained and unsanctioned absence from the palace. He would publicly decry that Nephele had deserted him and her children. She had forsaken them at a critical period of their lives, just as they approached adulthood with the celebrations of their sixteenth birthday. She had forsaken them, and it took all that he could do to console their youngest, Makistos, and comfort him as he grieved for his absent mother.

Athamas was fully committed to proving to Nephele and the whole kingdom that he didn't need her in his life anymore to be happy. In Ino, he would establish her as the new woman in his life, and his people will all be much happier with her as their queen.

Nephele was defunct, relegated to history. She had served a purpose and was now redundant.

He'd now focus all of his affections on Ino, as she was the future. His clarity and vitality would benefit because of her. His Kingdom would prosper all because he was invigorated once more.

***

Athamas called out from his office. 'Fetch me the merchant's assistant. The woman, Ino. Not Erastus.'

One of his aids stepped into his office and bowed. 'Yes, my lord,' he acknowledged, turned, and exited.

Athamas worked at his desk. He didn't like to be kept waiting and he was now especially impatient and irascible. He still hadn't spoken to the children since their mother had left. He was now concerned about what she had said to their children about her need for a hasty departure. Did she reveal details of how she had walked in on him enjoying sex with another woman. He wasn't certain how he would explain that.

They were sixteen and old enough to understand the significance of what he did and why their mother was upset with him. But he was also angry with her, because as the king, if he wanted sex with another woman, then that should be okay with everyone.

Elated with his reasoning, he spent the time reviewing the palace accounts. He enjoyed finding irregularities and worrying his chief exchequers' fiscal acumen with insightful questioning. It kept him on his toes and gave the man some sleepless nights, all of which amused Athamas.

There was a knock on the door.

'Enter,' he called out.

Ino cautiously entered the room.

'Come in, come in, please sit, make yourself comfortable, relax, it is so good to see you again,' he said trying to sound welcoming and friendly.

'You sent for me my lord?' she asked nervously. Ino refrained from his invitation to be seated. She had hoped there would be another person in the room as she feared a repeat of their last encounter.

'Yes! Please relax,' he again gestured for her to approach him at his desk. 'Please, be seated.'

She slowly sat down on the edge of the seat. She felt her heart rate was elevated. Her legs felt like they were ready to spring into action and she told herself that if he commanded sex, that this time she would flee the room and the kingdom. She would go home and marry someone of her parents choosing.

'Relax' he told her. He could sense her discomfort. 'I only wanted to talk with you.'

Ino tried in vain to relax. Erastus and Esmeralda had filled her head with numerous possibilities for her summons. She was more than a little afraid.

'Please, hear me out,' he pleaded. He desperately wanted to account his behaviour. 'I think it is important for you to know that I am truly sorry for the way I treated you. I clearly overstepped my position, and I feel that I have placed you in an awkward position. I ask that you will allow me to make amends and forgive me?' He looked at her imploringly in an effort to look like a lost boy who desperately needed her kindness. It was a technique that had produced beneficial results for him in the past.

Ino was puzzled. An apology wasn't postulated by her employers.

Athamas continued. 'Sometimes, as king, I forget myself. A man has needs after all. Not that that justifies what I did to you, of course!' he paused. 'It's just that, well things between my wife and I haven't been romantic for a long time now… and we haven't been intimate for a …' he mumbled weakly, and now felt he was failing to earn her sympathy and understanding. 'Did you know that she left me?'

'I did hear…' she answered.

'Well,' he interrupted her. 'It was probably for the best. Her seeing us like that probably did me a favour.'

'I beg your pardon.' She was even more confused.

'I know it was wrong and I said I'm sorry, but as it turned out, our tryst certainly helped me out of an unfortunate situation. My wife and I have grown apart, you understand, and well, I could explain it all to you, but it's a long, sad, boring story, and so I won't trouble you with it.'

She reluctantly relaxed into the chair. She was confused. On her previous visit, he had abused his position and coerced her into having sex with him. She knew it wasn't rape, but it also wasn't consensual. Him calling it a tryst, didn't make it a romantic rendezvous between consenting adults. She pondered, as his use of such words meant that he was convincing himself that she had wanted him in that way. He could even allude to others that she was being suggestive, perhaps promiscuous, and that she had a willingness to engage with him in that way. Many would believe him, and none would contradict his version of events. 'My lord, I appreciate your saying so and I hope you find happiness. For my part, you made it clear that I was to serve you. But I'm sure there are more experienced women that can...' she was unable to say it.

Athamas examined her in passive silence.

Ino quickly worried that she'd over stepped her response. She wanted him to understand that though he had the power to command her, that she'd prefer he chose a different woman.

'I don't think I'm making myself clear to you, Ino,' he replied softly.

Ino said nothing.

'I'm attracted to you. You are beautiful and smart,' he told her. 'I felt so comfortable when you were here last that I became attracted to you. Now, I find myself wanting our relationship to continue to blossom, and to grow and become something beautiful.

Ino still said nothing.

Athamas continued. 'I want you to stay here with me.'

She now frowned at him.

He added, 'I want you to move into the palace. I want you for my future wife. I want to make you happy and to be contented to become my queen.'

Ino was stunned. 'My lord...' she started to say.

He cut her off, 'I know it's sudden, and if you want a moment to think about it, I'd completely understand.'

'But my lord, you know nothing about me!' she exclaimed.

'Oh, I've done some research about you,' he informed her. 'Or, at least my staff have. You are the oldest daughter of Cadmus and Harmonia, King and Queen of Thebes. You are therefore a princess. Our marriage would be most appropriate and the people of Boeotia would love to have you as their queen and they would rejoice our union.'

Ino was stunned.

Athamas continued. 'We'll have some children together,' he told her. 'You do want to be a mother, don't you? Don't worry about Phrixus and Helle. They are sixteen and they won't need much mothering from you. Phrixus will soon begin his training to be a warrior prince and the protector of our realm. We won't see much of him. I'll marry Helle off to some handsome prince. That'll make her happy and keep her busy. I'm sure we can use her to form a useful alliance with a neighbouring kingdom.'

Ino stared at him.

'Do you accept?' he asked her.

'So, I'm to become the Queen of Boeotia?' she spoke softly, mostly to herself. Refusing him may be quite dangerous for her. He might kill her, or even worse, send her back to her parents as a disgraced soiled woman.

Athamas took her hesitation as a simple concern. 'Don't worry about Nephele either. As king I can confirm my own divorce. She's history.'

His explanation of his plans for them wasn't actually a marriage proposal in a loving sense. Ino couldn't believe what she was about to say. 'My lord.'

'Yes.'

'I'd be honoured to become your wife.'

He seemed relieved.

'May I show my gratitude?'

'Er, yes,' he wasn't sure what she intended.

She rose from her chair and walked up to him holding out her hand. He accepted it and stood up from his desk.

She led him into the back room and they re-engaged in his previous request. This time it was consensual.

***

Nephele had become comfortable living with Theophane and Chrysomallos. She was now participating eagerly in tending the gardens, and caring for the farm animals. She cooked and helped with cleaning. She and Theophane made some extra day clothes for Nephele to wear so that she could change daily and feel clean as well as safe.

After several weeks she began to get agitated and Theophane recognised the sign that it was time for Nephele to deal with her issues with her husband.

'I believe that you are planning to leave us soon, Nephele,' she said as she served each of them their evening meal.

'I think it's time I checked up on my children,' explained Nephele over her bowl of broth. 'With your permission, I now want to bring Makistos to live with me.'

'With us?' Theophane was willing, but their home was small.

'I'd like to build a home of my own, somewhere nearby. I now think of you as my family, and I'd appreciate Makistos enjoying a simple life with me here, close to you both.

'And the twins?'

'They are old enough to fend for themselves. They will be adults soon enough and Athamas has plans to raise Phrixus as his heir. It would be wrong on me to try to take that away from him. Helle will never leave her brother. They are tight-knit. She will be married off soon, to some man who will offer a significant dowry and a profitable benefit to his kingdom.'

'She should be allowed to marry out of love,' Chrysomallos ventured and Nephele smiled at his naivety.

'When will you leave?' Theophane asked.

'Tomorrow morning.'

Theophane was expecting this. She and Chrysomallos had discussed this eventuality. They shared a look and nodded. 'Chrysomallos will take you,' she informed her.

'Chrysomallos'? Nephele was confused. 'I accept that he is large for his age and strong too,' she added as Chrysomallos' chest and muscles swelled with male pride. 'But this could be dangerous. I wouldn't want to put him in any harm.'

'Now, Chrysomallos,' his mother instructed.

Chrysomallos stood up and dropped his cloak to the floor. Nephele was mesmerised as she watched the naked young man morph into an enormous ram with golden fleece. Next, large wings appeared on his flanks which he flapped by way of a demonstration. The air blew toward Nephele and she winced as if hit by a strong gust of wind.

Chrysomallos looked at Nephele and he spoke with a wry smile in his voice, 'I'll fly you to the palace. You can ride on my back.'

Nephele was stunned and somewhat lost for words.

'You'll need to carry his clothing in case he needs to change back into a man whilst you are with him,' stated his mother. 'It'll be safer if he does and less noticeable,' she added.

'I can carry them in a bag in my mouth,' added Chrysomallos, 'but then, I wouldn't be able to answer you, if you were to ask me a question.'

'Of course,' she replied expressing her understanding.

***

Later that night, as Theophane was getting ready for bed, Chrysomallos approached Nephele and asked in a hushed voice. 'Tell me more about the twins,' he asked.

Phrixus is strong, clever and resourceful. He will become the king one day and his father is already preparing him for that role.

'And Helle?'

What would you like to know about my daughter?' Nephele asked. She sported a knowing smile as it was only natural that he should have an interest in a girl of Helle's age.

'What is she like?'

'Tall, very beautiful, extremely clever. She's a great conversationalist.'

Chrysomallos nodded.

'She's resourceful and determined when she wants something. She knows what she likes and is generally good at getting her way.'

Chrysomallos smiled.

'She has long dark brown hair which is curly and she often looks a bit unkempt.'

'Unkempt?'

'You know, it looks untidy, not looked after. She loves me to brush her hair, but it doesn't stay straight for long, and then instantly it is all over the place again,' she motioned with her hands an outward expansion of hair as she explained, and then she laughed.

Chrysomallos laughed with her. He then leaned forward, wide eyed, as if to encourage her to continue talking.

'Helle is very inexperienced and a bit naive about the world,' Nephele cautioned. 'She has led a sheltered life. She'll need a man that is kind, and gentle, and compassionate to win her love and affections.'

Chrysomallos nodded knowingly. He now desperately wanted to be that man.

***

Sometime later Athamas happened to see the twins walking together in the passage way.

'Oh, by the way,' he said as he stopped them. 'I now consider myself divorced from your mother. She has abandoned the marriage and I'm free to make new arrangements for the benefit of the Kingdom. Don't worry, you place is secure. You'll remain heir to my throne Phrixus and will now start your training in the use of weaponry, and you'll be tutored on leadership and military strategy.

Phrixus grinned. He clearly accepted his father's plans for him.

'What will happen to me?' Helle asked.

'Soon I'll send word that I have a daughter of marrying age to the other kingdoms. We'll find you a suitable prince to marry.' He explained casually as it were a minor arrangement to make.

Helle immediately felt her tears welling. She had known all of her life that this was the probable fate for her, but she still dreamed of one day marrying for love, and not for the casual benefit of her father's kingdom.

'Oh, also I want you to know that I'm getting married soon. Her name is Ino. She is a lovely woman, a princess, but don't worry as she won't interfere in your lives. She wants her own children. I'll let you know the details soon, as I'm sure that you'll both want to be part of the wedding ceremony.' And with that announcement, their father, King Athamas turned and marched off. He exhibited a delightful gait in the way he moved. Their father was happy and that was always preferable.

The twins turned to each other, nodded and hastily returned to their chambers in stunned silence.

***

Later that night, brother and sister were consoling each other in the anteroom that they shared. It was situated between their bedrooms, and it served as a place where they could hold conferences about issues or opportunities when they needed privacy.

'I wish mother would come home soon,' said Helle.

'I wish we knew the truth about why she left,' added Phrixus. 'It must have been serious, as she would not leave us without a strong and compelling reason.'

'It was probably about sex and that new woman he plans to marry,' Helle stated flatly, she was deflated with the woes of her parents.

'Sex? What do you know of it,' asked Phrixus.

'I know enough. I also know that it causes problems between adults.

'I can't wait to try it,' Phrixus admitted.

'You already do it,' she revealed to him. 'And I know you enjoy it, and that you do it often, and that you are all alone when you do it,' she teased.

Phrixus's face flushed with embarrassment, 'I don't get many opportunities to meet girls.'

'You have me,' ventured Helle.

'You're my sister. I love you, but sex between us would be wrong,' he explained to her.

'I totally agree,' she answered. She loved her brother, but the thought of intimacy with him was repulsive. 'And it's not like I get to meet many boys either,' she added.

'Do you?'

'What?'

'Touch yourself, down there?'

"Of course not. That's disgusting,' she admonished. She blushed and hoped that she didn't give herself away. Of course she had, but she didn't want her brother to know about it.

Phrixus noticed her blush and immediately knew the truth about her. His imagination ramped up a notch. He suddenly felt that now would be an opportunity to explore her thoughts and desires. 'We could... if you wanted to,' he suggested hopefully.

'What?' she was puzzled.

'You know, do it. Just for a bit of fun, like learning a new game, for the experience.'

'Us, have sex?' Helle was incredulous.

'Just to see if we are any good at it.' Phrixus looked coy as his eyes widened. She had experienced that look from him all through her life. It mostly happened whenever her brother had decided that the two of them should do something that was risky, and that they would get into serious trouble if they were ever caught.

'No.' she shook her head. 'I've decided to save myself for the right man.'

'But, when that time comes, you won't know what to do. You'll embarrass yourself with your inexperience. At least with each other we can learn in a safe way, and we'll both avoid future humiliation.'

Her brother could be persistently persuasive when he wanted something from her. This time it was her body. She had seen him look at her in that way before, and that had always made her feel uncomfortable. Now she understood. It was as if he was undressing her with his eyes. She had sometimes thought that on those occasions, that he was spying on her while she bathed. Many years ago, they had bathed together, but since the growth of hair in the private areas, they had separated their ablutions. She was becoming increasingly concerned that his interest in her was starting to feel more and more like a violation.

'It would be a mistake to even discuss the possibility of sex between us. If father learned of your plan, he would become angry with you.'

'You wouldn't dare tell,' he replied calmly, knowing full well that she wouldn't. Their lifetime pact gave them permanent immunity from denouncing each other, regardless of the seriousness of the event.

'I won't, but the palace has ears and eyes. Anything as serious as sex between us would quickly become common knowledge.'

Phrixus could think of several places where they could consummate a sexual liaison that was away from the risk of exposure. He knew that if she shared his desire for intimacy, that she would also find a way so that they could do it. He therefore concluded that she was interested, but that she was stalling. So, he inwardly decided that he would continue to promote the benefits of them trying it with each other, just to learn more about sex, so that they were ready when the opportunity to do so with others presented itself.

Helle hoped that Phrixus was retreating from his idea, but she knew him well enough to know that it would only be a temporary cessation of his plan. Once he made up his mind that he wanted them to do something, he rarely gave up, irrespective of her views, or of the risks of discovery.

They sat in silence for a while, both pondering their next words. Then Phrixus reached over and placed his hand cupping Helle's exposed knee. 'I give you my promise that it won't hurt,' he said reassuringly, desperately wanting to allay any concerns that she may have. 'We'll take it slow, and be very gentle and careful.'

She pushed his hand away. She looked at him trying not to show her alarm. For their whole lives that had been inseparable. They had played, fought, wrestled, learned, and for much of their lives, they had even bathed together. Now, for the first time ever, when he touched her knee, she felt violated. Helle drew in a deep breath. 'I… I do not want to have sex with you Phrixus. I do love you, but not in that way. I'm in no hurry to learn such adult things, there is no rush, we are still young, and we have our whole lives to experience adult things when we are older.'

'I'm ready now.'

'Can't you find a nice girl in the village to have sex with? It doesn't have to be with me.'

'I don't want a filthy girl for sex.'

'She doesn't need to be a street whore. Just meet a nice girl, fall in love with each other and then it will naturally lead up to having sex. That's what I plan to do.'

'With a girl?'

'No silly, with a man. A compassionate man. One who is kind, and gentle, and loving. I want to feel like I am completely and unequivocally in love with the man that I give myself too.'

'I hate him already.'

Helle tried hard to suppress a smile.

Phrixus saw that she found his comment amusing and briefly laughed.

Helle laughed at his laugh, more out of relief that he was turning away from his incestuous desires. She was delighted that he was beginning to understand.

Phrixus laughed merrily. He was satisfied that she wasn't angry with him for revealing his desires for her. He knew she would keep it as their secret. He decided that he would wait until the right opportunity presented itself before he would try to have consensual sex with Helle in the future.

They calmed down and were now staring at each other when they were interrupted.

'What were you laughing about?' asked Nephele.

'Mother!' they exclaimed and rushed into her arms.

'How did you get in here?' Phrixus wanted to know.

She broke from their embrace. 'I'm sorry, but I can't stay long and I can't tell you much. I am sorrowful my darlings for all that is happening, but now is not the time to share the details with you.'

'Take us with you,' pleaded Helle.

'I can't. I am sorry. The time isn't right, and you'll be safer here, in the palace.'

'What about Makistos?' Phrixus asked about their much younger brother. 'He has been crying for you.'

'I know, and I will be taking him away with me tonight.' Then she added 'You both must stay here. How were your birthday celebrations. Did you enjoy yourselves?'

'Father cancelled them,' informed Phrixus.

'I'm sorry my darlings. I know you were looking forward to them. I'll see what I can do to change his mind,' she added.

'With all that is happening, we don't feel like celebrating,' Helle said sounding despondent.

'I'm sorry, my darlings.'

'He told us he is getting married.' Helle blurted. 'He is now planning his wedding celebrations.'

Phrixus added, 'He considers your departure a divorce.'

Nephele was silent.

'Did you leave because of her?' asked Helle.

'It seems that I must have,' she replied smiling. 'I just didn't realise how true it was at the time.'

She stood up ready to leave.

'When will we see you again, mother?' asked Phrixus.

'I'll return as soon as I can,' she assured them. 'Now don't follow me. I don't want your father to know how I got into the palace without being seen. He'll be angry enough when he learns I have taken Makistos.'

'But how...?' Phrixus wanted to know.

'I'll tell you more later,' she assured them. 'I love you both so much.' She held out her arms and they all embraced.

'What do we say to father?' Helle asked apprehensive.

'Remind him that I'm the cloud goddess. Tell him I came as a giant cloud and spoke with you and then whisked your brother away. It's close enough to the truth.

***

Athamas was furious when he learned of Nephele's visit. The children were cautious when explaining it to him. Phrixus had persuaded Helle that it would be wiser to tell their father themselves, before he learned of Makistos departure from servants or his nanny. He knew there would be anger, but he had hoped it wouldn't be directed at them.

'When did this happen?' demanded Athamas.

'Only a short while ago,' Phrixus lied. 'We came to you as fast as we could.'

Helle said nothing.

'Good, I'm pleased that you did,' then after a pause for thought, 'How did she get in without my guards seeing her?'

'She changed into a cloud and came to us in that way,' Phrixus explained.

'Yes, she could do that,' he paused then added. 'That fierce storm on the night that she left was her way of telling me that she was exceptionally angry,' he took a deep breath and sighed.

'What happened father?' Helle asked cautiously. 'Why would mother be so angry?'

'Your mother doesn't understand how my business negotiations are carried out. She thought I was being unreasonable in my dealings with the merchant that we use for the palace.'

Athamas was pleased with this explanation. He had prepared it in case they asked to know. 'In my opinion, I strike a fair and reasonable proposal when I do business.' Then he added, 'Your mother felt I wanted too much for what I was offering. We argued.' He paused, and then continued. 'She should not have interrupted my meeting.' Athamas went quiet. His children recognised that it was time to leave their father to his thoughts, and they motioned to each other that it was time to discreetly leave his room.

When they got to their own rooms Phrixus spoke first. 'I wonder what mother really discovered father doing when she interrupted his business meeting,' he speculated, but he thought he had a fair idea.

'I bet it has something to do with the reason why he is getting married so quickly,' Helle added.

'I wonder who he is marrying?' pondered Phrixus.

'I bet it will have something to do with him having sex,' Helle contributed.

***

Makistos had been overjoyed to see his mother and he had cried with relief when she picked him up and cuddled him. She packed some of his things, and then spirited them both back to where Chrysomallos was waiting for them. She positioned the boy in front of her as she settled on the rams back. 'I'm ready,' she told him and he flapped his wings and soon they were airborne and heading back home. Makistos was initially wide eyed with fear, despite his mother's constant reassurances that they were safe.

He was still a bit frightened when they landed, had a big drink of water which seemed to settle him, and then he snuggled himself into his mother's lap where he eventually fell asleep.

Later, Nephele settled Makistos into his new bed. As her son slept, Nephele described the events from the palace. She concluded with, 'My children are strong and brave, and I am completely proud of them.'

'I hope they'll be safe?' queried Theophane.

'I'll protect them,' added Chrysomallos.

Nephele laughed in delight. 'I think young Chrysomallos already has a crush on Helle,' she teased.

'Is that true?' Theophane asked him.

'We haven't even met yet,' he answered blushing. 'Nephele insisted that I remain hidden so that no one would learn of how we can get into the palace undetected.'

What will you do next? Theophane was serious.

'I believe Boeotia needs an extended period of glorious sunshine. That storm that I gave them when I left the palace might be the last rains they get for a long time,' she explained to them.

'But won't the people also suffer?' pleaded Theophane.

Boeotia has a wide, fresh water river flowing through it. It is fed from streams far away so there will be water for drinking and for the crops planted near the river's edge. I agree, that without rain the rest of the farming lands will quickly become parched. Athamas will be blamed for the drought and it will teach him not to mess with me!'

***

Greco was a regular caller to Erastus' business. Often, he'd spend the night with them as their house guest. The nature of the business they conducted was quite involved and often their discussions continued late into the evening. Greco had two strong competitive advantages over the others they did business with. Firstly, he was reliable. Secondly, he had access to products that originated far away from Boeotia. Over the course of several of his visits, Ino and Greco had begun to form a casual friendship. She enjoyed listening to him talk about his travels and learn of events that happened to people in far-away places.

The following morning, while Erastus and Esmeralda were still asleep, Ino and Greco breakfasted together and continued their conversation from the night before. Last night's business was conducted with large quantities of wine. However, both Ino and Greco were modest drinkers and they were both also early risers.

She was completing the payment to the travelling salesman. Often their business was conducted in trading goods, and this was good as it bolstered each other's inventories. On this occasion however, coins were also needed to complete the transaction, as Greco had many items that were in much demand in Boeotia and Erastus had ordered up big.

'Ino, there was a time when I thought that the two of us might have developed our friendship into something more intimate,' Greco said as he smiled warmly at her.

Ino had once thought the same, so she was careful in her reply. 'I'm exceedingly fond of you too, Greco,' but then she added, 'But now we'll never know what may have eventuated between us, as I'm now promised to marry the king.'

'Why do you continue to work here?' he asked.

'Oh, I enjoy it!' she answered with genuine enthusiasm. 'I get to meet interesting people like you.'

'That's great,' he said, but he seemed insincere. 'Will I ever see you again?'

'I hope so.'

'You'll miss your employers.'

'Erastus has taught me so much. Not just about business, but also about life!'

'He's a good man.'

'And Esmeralda is a good woman,' added Ino. 'They have sort of adopted me,' she sounded humble. 'When I first met them, it was at a seriously low point in my life.'

'Erastus told me your story,' Greco explained what he knew. 'He said, "giving you an apple on the day you met, was the best investment he ever made!"'

Ino blushed. 'I'd forgotten about that'.

'I'm leaving now,' he held up the bag of coins that she had counted out in front of him and smiled graciously. 'Our business is done, until next time. Give my best wishes to Erastus and Esmeralda and thank them once more for their custom and hospitality.'

'I won't be here when next you visit,' she came from around the work bench and kissed his cheek. 'You're a good and a kind man Greco. I wish you happiness.'

'I wish it to you also,' he turned to leave, but stopped. 'By the way, I have some cooking advice for you or Erastus and Esmeralda.'

'Oh?'

'Yes,' he laughed and then winced. 'My stomach hurts and I want to avoid this problem when I next eat with them. Ask them to gently roast the seeds and nuts before adding them to the meal. It improves their flavour and it'll stop the acid from hurting the tummy. Also, they'll last longer in storage as they won't germinate.'

'I'll tell them, thanks for the tip.'

'You're welcome,' he smiled, turned and exited the building.

Ino stood thinking about what Greco had told her. Seeds and nuts were always germinating when they got damp. A lot of stock got ruined in that way. If we lightly roasted them, as Greco suggested, then the seeds and nuts will last longer and we'll lose less of our inventory to spoilage. I bet we'll even be able to charge more for them too. I'll arrange for the workman to start work on roasting the seeds and nuts today. I'll even have it done for the palace stores also. The royal household will soon be my responsibility, and I might as well get started now. Ino was exceedingly pleased with herself.

***

Chrysomallos lay in his bed. He was thinking about Helle and couldn't sleep. He didn't realise that his feelings for her had grown so strong, until her mother had teased him about it. It was still many hours before dawn, so Chrysomallos decided that he would fly to the palace, find her, and bravely introduce himself.

Chrysomallos placed some of his best clothing into a cloth bag. He walked out into the dark night and got undressed. Away from the house he transformed into the mighty Ram with Golden Fleece and flapped his wings. He picked up the bag containing his clothes with his mouth and leapt into the air.

His flight to the palace was much quicker without Nephele on his back. He landed quietly on a balcony and looked about to confirm that he was unobserved. He changed back from being a Ram to being Chrysomallos the man, and quickly got dressed. He entered the palace. This area wasn't patrolled by the palace guards, as no-one ever anticipated a visitor, or an intruder, to come in this way. Even so, Chrysomallos was determined to be discreet and he moved about in earnest silence.

He first came upon the bedroom that was used by Phrixus. Glancing at him, he could hear that Phrixus was snoring. Satisfied that he was in a deep sleep, he silently left the bedroom, crossed the anteroom, and then carefully entered Helle's bedroom. He stared at her and realised that he was seeing his version of a sleeping beauty.

'Who are you?' her voice was only a whisper, but it made Chrysomallos jump in fright.

'A friend of your mothers,' he told her quietly.

Helle sat up turning her legs to the floor. She rose from the bed and crossed in front of the intruder and into Phrixus room. When she was satisfied that he was asleep, she returned to Chrysomallos and motioned him to follow her.

They walked down the passage and stepped into another room. Although it was dark, Chrysomallos could see that it was a room for learning. He examined the room and was fascinated with the books that filled the shelves and the parchments that lay on the writing desks.

'What are you doing here?' she asked. She didn't sound cross or even afraid that an intruder was in her home. She seemed more curious than concerned.

Chrysomallos was embarrassed to tell her that he simply came to look at her. He was surprised that they had this opportunity to properly meet, let alone speak with each other. She was more beautiful than he had imagined. Her soft voice was calming and almost musical, and he felt that he could listen to her speak forever. He was excited to meet her, but Helle took his manner to mean that he was scared.

'It's okay,' she consoled him. 'You don't need to be afraid. What is your name?'

'Chrysomallos,' he replied.

'Do you have a message for me from my mother?' she asked him kindly. She indicated that they should sit down.

He hadn't prepared for this, but it suddenly occurred to him of what to tell her. 'There will be a drought. There will be drinking water from the river, but the fields will become dry and the crops will be sparse.'

'Oh dear,' she looked sullen. 'For how long?'

'I don't know,' answered Chrysomallos.

'It's to punish father, isn't it?' she asked him.

'Yes, I think so.'

'Do you know what he did to upset my mother so much?'

'I don't know if I should tell you.'

'Was it something to do with sex?' she inquired.

'You know about sex?' he was surprised.

She laughed. 'I am sixteen,' she told him. 'I am a woman. Just because I haven't actually done it yet, doesn't mean I don't know how to do it.'

'I would like to, one day.' Chrysomallos was surprised by his own candour. He blushed.

'With me?' she asked in a kind way using her most gentle voice. She was smiling generously at him with youthful expectation.

'Yes,' he murmured. He was embarrassed and blushed even more. 'I mean… well you don't know me yet, but I feel I know everything about you and Phrixus. Your mother talks about you both so much. She lives with my mother and I, and well, I have sort of developed feelings for you. I know that sounds weird, but I already know that I always want to be with you.'

She studied him. He was beautiful. He was taller than her brother and more filled out. He was stronger, muscular, and his hair radiated a golden glow despite the darkness.

'Yes,' she told him. 'One day I think I'd like that.'

Chrysomallos whole body suddenly glowed and she laughed pleased at his excitement and the effect she was having on him.

'Helle, where are you?' Phrixus called to her.

'Toilet,' she called back. 'I'll be back soon.'

'Can you bring me some water?'

'I will.'

Chrysomallos had returned to his normal colour, his glow was diminished upon hearing her brother's voice.

He stood up. 'I had better leave,' he told her. 'It'll be getting daylight soon and I only fly at night.'

'You can fly!?' she whispered in urgent amazement.

'Yes, that's how I carried your mother here,' he explained. 'It is a secret, so please don't tell anyone.'

She shook her head and smiled in amazement. 'I have to go also. Please come back and tell me more about yourself. She reached up to him and hugged him and then gently kissed him on his lips.

Chrysomallos' whole body started to glow again.

'You'll have to learn to control that,' she told him with a grin on her face.

Chrysomallos said nothing. He was just grateful that his first meeting with this wonderful woman of his dreams had gone so well.

'Please return to me tomorrow night at the same time. Come directly to this room. I'll meet you here,' she explained, turned, went through the door, and was gone.

Chrysomallos waited a few moments and then he also left. On the balcony he took off his clothing and placed them into the bag. He became the flying Ram once more, picked up the bag in his mouth, and flew home. He had never been happier than he was at that moment.

***

The following night, after checking on his mother and Nephele that they were both in a deep sleep, Chrysomallos flew swiftly to the palace. He carefully threaded his way through the corridors and passed Helle's bedchamber. He went straight to the room Helle had told him to go into, and there he waited for her. He had no sooner sat down when he heard her come in the room.

She sat beside him and kissed him fully on the lips.

Chrysomallos started glowing and she laughed. 'You will certainly need to learn to control that,' she advised him.

I can't help it,' Chrysomallos admitted. 'You excite me,' he added. 'All I do is think of you. I know it is too soon to tell you how I feel about you, but it is true.'

'I may be inexperienced, and I may not understand relationships all that well, but you fit my imaginings of what it means to fall in love at first sight,' Helle explained. 'I hope that I am right about you?'

'Oh, you are,' he assured her. 'And, I have some gifts for you.'

Helle's face lit up. She almost glowed as much as Chrysomallos. She watched him as he reached into his bag and removed three magnificent pink roses. She accepted them by giving him a peck on the cheek. She watched him glow as she inserted them into her long curly hair above her forehead.

'How do I look,' she asked moving her head from side to side so he could admire her from all angles.

'Almost perfect.'

'Only almost?'

'Wear these, and you will be perfect.' He reached into his bag and removed a giant black pearl pendant which hung from a black neck band, and two magnificent black pearl earrings.

Her eyes lit up when she saw them. 'They are impressive,' she was ecstatic. 'Help me put them on.'

When they were in place he studied her. 'You are truly beautiful.'

'Do you know that I do feel beautiful when I am with you. You make me very happy.'

'I feel happy also, I'm so excited just to be near you.'

'I can tell,' she smiled staring directly at the obvious bulge in his clothes. 'Is that another present for me? May I see it?'

Chrysomallos hesitated for a brief moment, and then he stood up, pulled down his pants, and sat beside her. He was visibly aroused.

Helle lifted up her skirt and reached for Chrysomallos hand. She guided him to her womanly parts. Chrysomallos glow intensified.

'May I touch yours?' she asked him.

'Yes please,' he whimpered.

She held his shaft and gently tugged on it when he suddenly ejaculated a stream of warm fluid over her hand and up her arm.
'I'm so sorry,' he pleaded.

Helle chuckled with amusement. 'Don't be sorry, Chrysomallos. I think that's the biggest compliment anyone has ever given me.' She smiled reassuringly and leaned forward to kiss him again. Their lips met hungrily.

'I think we'd better clean you up,' she told him.

There was a wash basin with water from a decanter.

She rinsed her arm and hands. She next washed him and he began to stiffen once more with an accompanying glow about his body.

'Down boy,' she told him gently. 'I think we've done enough for one night.'

Chrysomallos reluctantly agreed. The glow subsided as he got dressed.

She kissed him once more. 'I'm really looking forward to you putting that inside me.'

'Me too,' he mumbled

'We'll make perfect babies together one day.'

'Yes.' He never before felt so desperately in love.

'You'd better go now,' she explained reluctantly, 'Before we get caught.

Chrysomallos agreed, kissed her once more, and then left the room. At the balcony, he disrobed and then flew home with love in his heart.

Helle was about to return to her bed when she was confronted by Phrixus. 'You smell of sex,' he accused her.

'Do I?' she retorted. 'How would that be possible?'

'I don't know' he replied, 'But it is the same smell that I have when I …' his voice trailed off.

'But I can't do that,' she informed him. 'I don't have a penis.'

'I know, so…?' he was bewildered.

'Count sheep, and go to sleep,' she advised him. She got into bed and pretended to sleep.

***

The wedding ceremony between Athamas and Ino was brief. There were only a few special guests at the banquet. They included Erastus and Esmeralda who were in two minds about being there. They were behind Nephele's meeting with the king, but now she was replaced by Ino, who was also their responsibility. Though they had no influence over the circumstances of their king's relationships, they felt that they were at the forefront of all of the unfolding drama.

There were a couple of speeches thanking some of the gods for this and that. No one made reference to the belief that there was now a drought, although all the guests had heard a rumour and it seemed that it had been a long time since they had experienced rainfall. They politely kept any concerns to themselves.

Ino was clothed beautifully in a dress that was a wedding gift from Erastus and Esmeralda. Before the wedding, Esmeralda fussed over her the same way a devoted mother would have done for her daughter on her special day. Ino was pleased for her administrations and affections.

Ino was also relieved that Athamas had not invited her parents. She thought that he might, in some show of reconciliation between her and them. She wasn't ready for that, and was grateful that she didn't have to deal with them, yet.

Ino was concerned about the news that the palace seed and nut stock had been poisoned. She herself had arranged for those stocks to be lightly roasted. It seemed like a good idea at the time, as it would save spoilage and germination. As it transpired, that stock was seed stock and was destined to be planted in the fields. The roasting had now made that impossible. The rumour mill had it that Nephele was responsible for this outrage, and Ino was relieved about that.

A few staff knew the truth that the seed and nut stocks were roasted under her orders, and she was concerned about that becoming public knowledge. She didn't know if Athamas knew what she had done, but if he did, he kept it to himself. It seemed that the palace staff knew better than to discuss what they knew with anyone, and she was relieved about that. She was glad that Nephele was being blamed. She was sorry to think that the stock was thought to have been poisoned, as it was perfectly fine to eat, and she hated to see food go to waste.

Ino was also concerned about the twins. They were at the ceremony of course, but they didn't warm to her. Admittedly this was only the second time she was with them, and of course, everyone was busy with the wedding. Their first meeting was quite brief and when the twins were told that she, Ino would become their new mother, she noticed they both winced. Ino thought that she must have winced also, as she hadn't figured on being a mother to Nephele's brats. She was only glad that Nephele had seen to it that the toddler was no longer here, as that was something she didn't want to have to deal with.

She wondered if these mixed emotions were typical of a bride on her wedding day. She hoped they were, but she also concluded that her situation was different from traditional weddings.

During the ceremony, Ino mumbled her consent when required, and wore a smile when she noticed she was being watched, which was all the time. Why were brides supposed to look so damn happy all the time? She was being sentenced to a lifetime pleasing her man, a king no less. She'd have to survive the political manoeuvrings with the nobles of Boeotia, run the palace and their staff, and deal with his two unwelcoming teenage children. It then occurred to her that he may want her to give birth to his children also! That was an unpleasant thought. It didn't seem that there was much to smile about. At least she wouldn't have to cook, as she despised cooking as much as she hated cleaning.

Some people were coming to congratulated them, and so she reinvigorated her smile. She mumbled her thanks and gratitude.

'You are a beautiful bride, my darling.'

Ino turned to see who it was that was speaking about her. It was her husband! 'Thank you,' she replied with forced enthusiasm.

'What more can we do to make this day even more special?' he pondered out aloud.

You could arrange to have your children murdered, thought Ino. But she said nothing.

'You have a lovely smile my bride, but your eyes give you away,' he observed, and then added. 'What troubles you?'

'The children don't seem pleased about our marriage,' she told him.

'It's to be expected. They didn't choose you; I did. They will learn to be respectful. I can't envisage that they'll love you the way I do, but we can't have everything, can we?' he smiled and she smiled back working on doing so with her eyes also.

He laughed.

Ino said nothing.

'Phrixus, Helle! Come here please.' he called out summoning them.

Both stopped what they were doing and came to their father and stepmother. 'Yes father,' they chorused.

'Have you congratulated your stepmother yet?' he asked them.

'Of course!' they lied in unison. In turn, they hugged Ino.

'Phrixus. You are almost a man,' his father told him, 'I hear your training and education are going well, and that you are skilled with sword, spear, and also cunning with words. A man who can think on his feet and meld to the ever-evolving circumstances, has a distinct advantage over others.'

'Thank you, father,' Phrixus replied. 'The trainers you selected for me are the best, they motivate and inspire me to one day emulate your example,' he said returning the compliment.

Athamas laughed contentedly. 'You'll now commence a more intensive training. I want you in my personal counsel. You will learn what it means to be a king,' Athamas informed him.

'Thank you, father,' Phrixus sounded pleased.

'Helle.'

'Yes father.'

'You're a beautiful young woman and I hear you have admirable intelligence to go with it.'

'Thank you, father.'

'We'll now commence a search to find you a suitable husband,' he told her.

Internally Helle was reeling, but she managed to blurt out yet another, 'Thank you, father'.

Ino winced at her own memory of what was once planned for her. In hindsight, it may not have been such a bad thing, but she knew what the poor girl was now thinking. But what did she care? It'll get Helle away from here and the sooner the better.

'I'll be only too pleased to help you my dear,' Ino told Helle.

I bet you will, thought Helle. 'I'm grateful for all the help you can give me,' she replied smiling. Ino noticed the smile was not her eyes and inwardly laughed at the hypocrisy of this new family pantomime.

Phrixus and Helle excused themselves and returned to their friends. Athamas didn't realise they had any, but he was distracted from continuing that thought by The Oracle.

The Oracle was a distinguished man in the community. Many people trusted and even revered the man. He was uncannily accurate with forecasts and predictions.

Few realised that he was wealthy also as he was well paid by the people for his counsel. He was known only as "The Oracle", and he was consulted by anyone whom could afford him, even the king.

'My king,' said The Oracle. 'You choose not to consult me about your intended bride,' he stated maintaining his smiling demeanour.

'I didn't consult you about my first bride either,' Athamas replied smiling.

'And you won't consult me about your third bride either,' The Oracle said smilingly back at him.

Athamas scowled but said nothing.

The Oracle continued. 'The boy will be trouble. He doesn't respect you or like your bride. Whilst he lives, the drought will continue. Nephele is a powerful enemy.'

'Oh.'

The Oracle continued. 'The word on the street is that Phrixus physically coerced poor Chiara for her sexual favours. Her family is now getting ready to make trouble for you and they will seek justice. It's best to get rid of him.'

'Chiara?'

'She is that young woman that Phrixus now stands with. She doesn't know it yet, but she is bearing his child. He'll soon find out about her condition, and her parents will demand either a wedding, or a significant compensation. The people will side with them against you. Both outcomes will lead to his ruin.'

Athamas studied his son. He was talking with a young woman that Athamas hadn't seen before. She appeared to be elegant, and he could understand his son's interest in her. He now wished that he had spent more time teaching him the intricacies of women.

He turned to face The Oracle. 'And Makistos?'

'He is lost to you. Make yourself a new son. Do it soon.'

'And my daughter?' he asked The Oracle.

'I advise you to marry Helle off quickly. Don't fuss with who, as long as they live far away from here,' the Oracle advised him.

'I appreciate and respect your wisdom, Oracle,' he paused. 'How much do I owe you?'

The Oracle looked at him blankly. 'Consider it a wedding present,' he turned and left.

The Oracle gave Ino a very subtle knowing nod as he walked past her.

Ino gave herself an inward smile. She now felt she was in control once again and this pleased her. The large bag of gold coins she had paid The Oracle was clearly a good investment.

***

Several days later, Chrysomallos once more landed on the balcony of the palace. Nephele alighted from his back and Chrysomallos morphed back into a man. She handed Chrysomallos his clothes. Chrysomallos had never felt uncomfortable being naked in front of her. He dressed quickly.

Nephele spoke softly to Chrysomallos. 'Follow me,' she instructed him.

Chrysomallos said nothing.

Chrysomallos followed Nephele into the palace. They were soundless and Chrysomallos observed her checking that the way was clear for both of them at every turn.

Chrysomallos feigned interest in where they were going and looked about with curiosity when arriving at the bed chambers of Nephele's teenage children.

Nephele shook Phrixus shoulders to gently wake him up. Silently, she motioned for Phrixus to follow her into Helle's room.

Phrixus noticed his sister's reaction when she saw Chrysomallos standing in the room. She beamed with delight.

Chrysomallos stifled a glow.

Phrixus glared at Chrysomallos. Nephele didn't see her son's reaction to seeing Chrysomallos there. Helle was pleased to see her mother and she hugged her with unabashed enthusiasm.

'Who is this?' Helle asked looking at Chrysomallos.

Phrixus almost gagged at the hypocrisy of it all.

'This is Chrysomallos,' Nephele introduced her children to the man standing shyly beside her.

'Chrysomallos, this is my daughter Helle, and my son Phrixus.'

Chrysomallos nodded at both of them. He had noticed that Phrixus pulled an angry face when Helle looked at him, but said nothing. Now he worried that he knew about what was happening between him and his sister. It seemed to him that he must. Could Helle have told him, he doubted that. Perhaps he had been spying on them?

Nephele was too busy making arrangements to notice the awkwardness between the teenagers. 'Tomorrow, Chrysomallos will come here on his own. He will fly you both to safety,' Nephele explained to them.

'What do mean, fly?' asked Phrixus suspiciously.

'Chrysomallos has a special gift,' she told them. 'He can transform himself into a giant Ram with wings. He is strong enough to carry you both away from this place.'

'A flying sheep!?' Phrixus almost yelled with the incredibility of it all.

'I would show you, but I'd have to be naked first,' Chrysomallos stated. He noticed Helle's smile and suppressed a glow.

Nephele continued, 'I have learned that Ino has been actively plotting against both of you. I have heard that she has convinced your father that you are both trouble for him. She has even suggested that you should both be sacrificed to the gods. Many people believe that with your death, that it will bring rain and end the drought.'

'But he told me that I was to be educated to work with him in his inner counsel,' Phrixus explained, defending his father.

'And he told me that they would find me a suitable husband,' Helle added.

Chrysomallos stiffened.

'They are all lies, deceit and trickery,' Nephele warned them.

'How do you know these things mother?' Phrixus asked.

'I still have many friends in the palace,' she told him.

'When we have gone from here, will you end the drought?' Helle asked. Her concern always went beyond her own needs.

'I promise you, that when you are safe that I'll end the drought.' She smiled and Helle smiled back at her, pleased with this commitment.
'Where will we go mother?' Helle asked.

Arrangements have been made with Chrysomallos' grandfather. His name is Aeetes, and he lives in Colchis. He will welcome you all at his palace until I can join you there.

'What about Chrysomallos?' asked Phrixus.

'Chrysomallos and his mother will join us also in Colchis. Chryso-mallos mother, Theophane, is the daughter of Aeetes and grand-daughter of Helios. We have powerful allies,' she advised them proudly.

'Chrysomallos, are you certain you can carry both of us?' asked Helle.

'I am an immensely massive and powerful Ram,' he assured her with a wink of his eye, but he thought that perhaps she had missed it.

Helle nodded, seemingly reassured.

'Chrysomallos. Go to the balcony and wait for us. We'll follow shortly so that they can see where to meet you when you come tomorrow.'

Chrysomallos looked at them all, nodded, and then exited.

'He is a good man,' added Nephele.

'A ram of a man,' mocked Phrixus.

'Phrixus, if you choose to remain here with your father, you'll face a certain death. Chrysomallos will rescue both of you.'

Nephele turned and led the way to the balcony that she and Chrysomallos had been landing on. She demonstrated her discreet method of moving from room to room, being vigilant against being seen by guards or palace staff. Fortunately, they were all asleep, and so they reached the balcony unobserved.

Chrysomallos was already once more in his male sheep form. His bag of clothes hung from his mouth. Nephele took the bag from him and climbed onto his back.

'I love you both my darlings,' she told them. 'We'll be reunited soon.'

Helle hugged her mother, but Phrixus held back. He didn't approve of these new arrangements. He despised Chrysomallos for the obvious love that Helle felt for him. He was right about her, and he was now convinced that she even had had sex with him. It wasn't fair, she was his.

He also resented his mother for revealing his demise, especially when he, until now, believed his father that he was to inherit the throne. His world was falling apart and he hated everyone for it.

Also, Chiara had asked to meet him. He knew what he did to her was wrong, but he was the prince, a future king, and she should have respected his needs and understood his privileged position. Maybe she had reconciled her feelings toward him, and now realised that he was the best thing that had ever happened to her. Perhaps she even wanted to feel him inside of her again. It was even possible that Chiara now dreamed of becoming his queen one day. That would give him leverage over her behaviour and willingness. He smiled at the power he felt. He then frowned. Leaving the palace with Helle on the back of a flying ram was going to ruin everything.

Chrysomallos flapped his wings and leapt into the air.

The twins watched their mother astride Chrysomallos back. They grew smaller with the distance they quickly covered.

'A flying sheep. Who'd would have guessed that my sister would have fallen in love with a flying sheep.'

'He's a Ram,' defended Helle.

'But, does he perform for you as a man or as a ram?' mocked Phrixus making the disgusting motions of sex as they returned to their bed chamber.

'I sometimes have no idea what you are talking about, Phrixus.' Helle told him without malice.

***

The following morning, Phrixus rose early, washed, dressed, ate, and left the palace, all without Helle knowing of his activities.

He was on a mission to learn if what his mother had told them was true. Before he abandoned a promised idyllic life as a prince and future king, he wanted to learn if the threats were real.

He found Chiara working in her father's fruit and vegetable outlet. It was early and they weren't busy. She visibly stiffened when she saw him, but at the same time she was grateful that he had come.

'Chiara,' he said as he approached.

'Not here,' she cautioned. 'Follow me.'

He followed her past the numerous crates of assorted fresh fruits and vegetables that were yet to be put on display. He grabbed an apple, as was his right, and took a healthy bite from it as he followed the young woman to a private room. The room had some chairs positioned around a table. It looked as if it doubled as an office and a lunch room. The sat facing each other.

'My father knows,' she explained, her voice barely above a whisper.

'Why did you tell him?' he asked, trying desperately to appear unconcerned.

'He monitors my cycle. I'm overdue. He confronted me and I had to tell him. I also told him that you truly loved me.' And with that she smiled hopefully.

'Why did you do that?' Phrixus was puzzled. He was rapidly feeling cornered.

'Would you rather I told him that you raped me?' she mocked, but there was venom in her voice.

Phrixus went pale. He thought a rape allegation would be his word against hers, and that he might be believed because of his father. But the shadow of doubt would hang over him for life. He swallowed before he spoke. 'I do love you,' he mouthed, but it didn't sound convincing even to his own ears.

She smiled at him hiding her contempt. 'My father now expects that you will declare your love and devotion for me publicly.'

'Yet, my father may have other plans for me. Your father should be careful, he may be jeopardising your families standing within this kingdom.'

This time it was Chiara that went pale. She looked up when she noticed that someone was entering the room. Before Phrixus could react, Chiara's father had come behind Phrixus and now held a long blade to his throat. His other hand rubbed the teenage prince's chin.

'I can feel some stubble, Chiara. Your boy is becoming a man.'

Phrixus turned white with fright. He recognised the voice and knew that he was being held by Chiara's father. He truly believed that he was now in some serious trouble.

'I think perhaps I should use this blade to give you a shave. After all, you do want to look presentable when you meet the rest of the family to announce your betrothal.'

Phrixus felt the urge to urinate. Tears now welled in the corners of his eyes. He was genuinely frightened.

'What do you think, Chiara. Do I shave or should I cut?' he asked trying to sound sincere.

'Shave.'

'Do we have an understanding young prince?'

'Yes.'

'Good.' The shave was barely enough to make a difference. When the father was finished, he stood the boy up, turned him toward the door and pushed him toward it. 'They are all eager to hear your announcement.'

The father motioned for his daughter to follow them, and they all went to the courtyard that was used for significant family gatherings. The father yelled for all to bear witness to the announcement.

Chiara stood next to Phrixus. If she knew that her father held the point of the blade onto his back, she didn't show it, or she didn't care.

'Phrixus, son of King Athamas, future ruler of Boeotia, has a pleasing announcement to make, he explained to a gathered group of expectant faces. Everyone was smiling and seemed genuinely please with the situation.

Phrixus drew in a deep breath. He hesitated when he spied some of the palace staff walk into the area. They were unarmed so it wasn't a rescue.

'We welcome the honoured guests from the Kings court to witness these events,' Chiara's father clearly had enough influence to ensure that his father would quickly learn that he was becoming engaged to a commoner.

Chiara leaned over and kissed him, much to the delight of the onlookers. Phrixus felt he was doomed. He felt the knife press on his back. He drew in another deep breath and finally uttered the words that he knew the gathered people wanted to hear. 'I am proud to announce our happy betrothal between the beautiful Chiara and myself.' The crowd erupted in cheers. Phrixus relaxed. He had uttered the words that spared his life and would give him time to work a plan to escape marrying this girl.

He silently endured the breakfast feast that followed. He shook hands with numerous strangers, and several ugly old women came and hugged him and kissed him. He felt dirty, and he wanted to run away, but Chiara held his hand firmly and he knew that her father and four brothers were never far away.

When the opportunity came, he explained softly to his intended that he must now go an explain their plans to his father, the king. They kissed, parted, and with a nod to her family, he left their company.

As he walked, he found himself crying like a small child. Phrixus already knew that telling his father of the mess he was in wasn't an option. He reluctantly decided that he would travel with Helle on the back of a flying Ram. He would escape matrimony with a woman he didn't know or love. He would flee from the fallout that would happen when his father was apprised of what he had done.

At least he'd still be with Helle.

***

That night, at the agreed time, Chrysomallos once more landed gently on the balcony of the palace.

Phrixus had already been hiding on the balcony, mostly to avoid escalating the disastrous turn of events with his forced engagement to Chiara, and to escape his father's anger, but also to confront the man who had won the heart and love of his beautiful sister.

After Chrysomallos dressed, he sat beside the man he considered would become his future brother-in-law.

'Good flight?' Phrixus asked, initiating conversation.

'Uneventful.' Chrysomallos smiled.

'You've done this journey many times,' alluded Phrixus.

'I have, you must understand, Helle is very special to me, she is worth the risk, just being with her.'

'How many times have you... been together?'

'Four,' Chrysomallos replied innocently.

'And you have been familiar with her every time?' Phrixus asked, trying desperately to keep his voice conversational, despite a growing urge to enact some form of retribution toward this man for violating his beloved sister.

Chrysomallos' unabashed boyish grin confirmed his worst fears.

'You love her!' Phrixus declared.

'He had better,' Helle's voice startled them both. They hadn't heard her approach.

Chrysomallos stood up to greet her and she gave him a loving embrace and an overly passionate kiss. She did this both to please her lover, but also to demonstrate to her brother that all of her affections were for Chrysomallos.

Chrysomallos glowed.

Phrixus seethed, but he said nothing.

'How will you know which direction to go. Isn't harder to see in the dark?' Helle was concerned.

'I'll head for Selene as she will be my guiding light.'

The twins looked at the moon and understood that she was due east, and in the direction that they were headed. Chrysomallos knew what he was doing.

'We should go,' Chrysomallos advised. He stepped back and disrobed. Helle had allready seen him naked on several occasions but she still delighted in seeing him in this way. She looked forward to being in his lovers embrace once more.

Phrixus was surprised at the man's member. He felt intimidated by it and the thought that he had wielded it to being sexual with his beloved sister angered him. He fumed in silence, aware that any hostility might deny him a ride on the Rams back and safely take him away from his mounting problems.

Chrysomallos asked, 'If you could carry the bag for me, please? It's easier to fly without it in my mouth and we can talk on the way.'

Helle took the bag of clothes from him and hugged his neck. The twins watched in fascination as he changed into the Ram once more.

Phrixus looked on as his sister with a wry smile on his face. 'How should we do this?' Phrixus asked. 'Who gets on first?'

The Ram told them. 'Helle, you climb on first. Be sure not to strangle my neck and get in the way of my wings. Phrixus, you climb on behind Helle and hold onto her waist.

'What do I hold onto?' asked Helle.

'Hold onto the wool on the side of my neck.'

They climbed on and adjusted themselves. All three were nervous. For Chrysomallos this was the heaviest load that he'd had ever carried.

They had previously discussed him carrying them one at a time, but Nephele was worried about Helle being left alone at the palace or at Colchis.

Chrysomallos initially struggled, but slowly he gained height. He turned toward Colchis and pumped his wings to gain height and speed. He felt the tight grip of Helle on his wool. He smiled happily at the thought of the two of them being together forever.

Chrysomallos explained, 'I won't go too high,' he assured them.

Phrixus and Helle said nothing.

'And don't look down,' Chrysomallos added.

'My eyes are closed,' Helle called back.

Phrixus also had his eyes shut tight but he said nothing. He held onto Helle's waist as if his life depended on it.

Initially, the flying gave them an adrenalin rush. Soon the land beneath them had given away to ocean. They eventually began to relax and settle in the rhythm of the flight. It seemed to them they were flying for ages. The beating of the wings was almost hypnotic and both Phrixus and Helle were struggling to stay alert, despite the danger.

They had discussed the advantages flying over land but had dismissed it. The distance that way would be three times longer and the risk of being seen was much greater. They needed the twin's disappearance to become a mystery.

Chrysomallos pumped his wings and continued flying into the night. He knew he was getting weaker, but just knowing the love of his life was sitting on his back gave him the strength and the energy to continue.

Helle was also exhausted from holding on for so long. She wondered about Chrysomallos. She was worried that he must be getting tired when she felt that her brother's hands were now moving up her torso and were now cupping her breasts. She let go of the fleece with one hand and moved his hands back down her waist. But as soon as she held back onto the fleece, his hands were moving back up, this time he was gently kneading her breasts. 'Phrixus! Please! Stop doing that!'

'What's happening?' Chrysomallos asked in concern.

'Phrixus is fondling my breasts!'

'What, why?' Chrysomallos demanded and he swung his head to try to see. The movement shifted their weight and they almost lost their balance.

But Phrixus just laughed and continued. He moved his hands under her bodice and he was now teasing each nipple with his fingers. He was pressing his groin into her back and he was moving rhythmically against her. She felt his erection swell pressing against her. She reached behind her to hit it so that he would become dissuaded by this unwanted and inappropriate behaviour. As she swung her body toward him, she completely lost her balance and began sliding away from the rams back. She screamed in terror.

'Helle!' Phrixus screamed. Phrixus locked his knees into the Ram's flank whilst reaching down desperately with his arms extended trying to grab her. He tried to hold her hands, but his grip failed him, and she slid off the Ram and fell toward the dark waters below.

Chrysomallos looked down to see his beloved Helle falling beneath them. He had felt the sudden decrease in weight on his back.

She was screaming in blind panic.

He swooped down desperately trying to catch her on his back.

Helle's fall was over quickly. She thudded into the ocean with a loud sickening splat, and then she sank beneath the waves. The night's darkness was masking her blood which was now mixing in with ocean water.

Chrysomallos circled the area where she impacted. The moon light was scattered by the clouds and neither of them could see any sign of her.

Chrysomallos reluctantly told her brother that they would have to continue without her. If they didn't continue, they may both drown also.

Phrixus said nothing as Chrysomallos once more turned for Colchis, flapping his wings to regain height.

After about an hour they finally came to land. Chrysomallos landed and changed to his human form. His clothing was lost with Helle, but he was too exhausted to worry about that. Both young men collapsed on the sand up from the shore and slept.

Dawn awoke them. Chrysomallos noticed that Phrixus had been crying and felt the tears well up in him also.

Phrixus's grief slowly turned to anger. 'You could try to find her.'

'She is gone.' Chrysomallos told him. 'Smashed and drowned.'

'You don't know that for certain. She may have survived,' he wanted to believe. 'She may have swum to shore.'

'I loved her too you know.' Chrysomallos knew of Phrixus inappropriate sexual behaviour and that it had led to Helle's death. Despite this, he was trying to be sympathetic.

'Not like I did!' Phrixus yelled. 'We were inseparable for sixteen years,' he continued.

'I'm sorry she fell. I know that you wanted a sexual relationship with her. She told me about it.'

'I didn't! I'm her brother.'

'But you were fondling her breasts as we flew?' Chrysomallos might have been naive, but he was catching on quickly. 'You were violating her and she fell to her death trying to escape from you.'

'I'm sorry!' he continued after a pause. 'Please, I beg you. Go and have a look for her. She might...'his voice trailed off.

Chrysomallos said nothing.

'Please,' Phrixus implored. 'You said you loved her. Prove it!'

'I should go and find her, so that you will be punished for your crimes against her. I know that my word alone against yours will fail, but together we will prosecute you,' Chrysomallos promised as he commenced his transformation once more into the winged ram.

The Ram turned to face Phrixus when he saw a knife in Phrixus' hand flash toward him. He didn't have time to react, and the blade cut through the Ram's neck spilling torrents of blood onto the sand.

As the blood pumped out, quickly draining Chrysomallos life force with it, Phrixus told him calmly, 'I hold you fully responsible for Helle's death. You will now rot with Hades.'

And so, laying on the sand before him, Chrysomallos died.

Phrixus heard noises behind him. He turned in alarm, the bloodied knife still in his hand.

'Peace friend,' said the man standing before him. 'A good kill, by the look of things,' the man said and was referring to the dead ram laying before them.

'Yes,' replied Phrixus now realising he wasn't in any danger or trouble.

'It is an enormous beast. What will you do with it?' asked the man.

'I…' hesitated Phrixus.

'Will you eat it?' the man asked him.

'I don't know,' Phrixus replied softly.

'It's a shame to waste it. That fleece will be quite valuable too.'

Phrixus realised that he didn't have any coin. By killing Chrysoma-llos, he didn't have any transport either. He didn't know how much farther he had to travel to Colchis.

Finally, Phrixus offered the man a bargain. 'If you could help me skin him, I'll be pleased for you to have the meat.'

'It is a deal,' the man replied reaching for Phrixus's hand and shaking on it. 'I have many mouths to feed.'

The man knelt beside the ram and produced a sharp knife. He expertly gutted the ram and peeled off the fleece. 'The blood will wash off,' he explained to Phrixus who watched the man work in quite amazement. He realised this man had done this before.

The Golden Fleece was now removed from the Ram's body.

'Wash it in the ocean,' the man instructed him.

Phrixus dragged the fleece to the water's edge and worked the blood off the wool. The cleaner it was, the more impressive the

Golden Fleece became. The sunlight was bright and the Golden Fleece was now dazzling.

The man now had the ram's carcass slung over his shoulders. 'Come with me,' he invited Phrixus. 'We'll clean you up, feed you, and then I'll send you on the correct path.'

Phrixus gathered the Golden Fleece into a bundle and also placed it over his shoulders. He followed the man off the beach and into his encampment. There were some other men and some women, and lots of children.

Phrixus was on his guard despite their friendliness. They gave him a meal and some provisions in a tote bag to take with him. They also gave him another bag, large enough and strong enough to carry the Golden Fleece. They showed him how to carry it as a giant back-pack.

'That's a valuable asset,' the man cautioned him. 'Be cautious to who you show it to.'

They pointed him in the direction of Colchis and advised him he should be able to walk there in two days.

***

After several days of hopeful waiting, both Nephele and Theophane were now convinced that their children had met with disaster.

Chrysomallos had not returned as arranged.

Nephele had gone to the palace disguised as a cloud and had learned that the twins had mysteriously disappeared. No one spoke about Chrysomallos, so she was able to assure Theophane that he must have collected them, but that sadly, there was no other news.

Four days later Poseidon arrived. He explained that to Theophane and Nephele that he had heard of a woman named Helle had fallen from the sky and into the ocean, and that sadly she had drowned. He explained that he wasn't in that location at that time, and so he couldn't save her. It was apparent to Poseidon that both women were in mourning, and that they were in no mood for his company, so he waved his farewell and departed.

The two women continued to live together and they focused on raising Makistos. They renamed him, Macistus, to hide his identity from his father. The boy had a good life, especially when he was happily playing with their dog in the garden, or exploring the coastline. He grew up to be educated, kind, resourceful, and as a man he was a solid and much respected citizen.

Many years later, the town Macistus, was named after him.

***

Athamas was both relieved and disappointed at the departure of his children. He concluded that they had run away to avoid the plans that he had for them. It was just as well.

Ino was soon pregnant. Over the years she bore him two male children, who were named Learches and Melicertes. Ino spent little time with them, and they were raised in separate quarters by nannies and tutors.

The people were not agreeable with his choice of bride, and Athamas and Ino soon drifted apart. "That damn Oracle" thought Athamas. He realised that The Oracle had put the power of suggestion into his mind when he had told him that their marriage wouldn't work. Combined with the knowledge that it was Ino that that had ordered the seeds and nuts to be roasted, thereby rendering them useless for the crop, he had concluded that he would one day divorce her also.

In a fit of madness Athamas killed Learches during a hunting trip. He became enraged, and in fear for their lives, Ino and their other son, Melicertes fled by jumping into the ocean. As they were never seen again, Athamas conclusion was that they had drowned, but Ino survived and had actually managed to escape his madness.

In the years that passed, Ino turned to Dionysus for comfort. Dionysus is the god of wine and was responsible for the deplorable behaviour of persons under his influence. She consumed it in great quantities. Ino joined a group of women who were known as the Maenads. They were permanently in Dionysus' embrace.

Athamas eventually remarried. He and Themisto had four children together. Athamas eventually learned the truth about Ino, and during a phase of deep regret he tried to rekindle their relationship. Themisto became angry and very jealous. For Athamas, the tragedy continued when Themisto attempted to have Ino's remaining child assassinated, but Ino managed to thwart her plot, and in a case of mistaken identity, Themisto's own children were killed instead. In her grief, Themisto took her own life.

***

Phrixus had a long but uneventful journey to the city. King Aeetes of Colchis greeted Phrixus with a warm and loving embrace. The King was the son of Helios the God of the sun. He was father to Theophane and Grandfather to Chrysomallos. He glowed when he met Phrixus, but the glow quickly diminished when he learned the fate of his grandson, Chrysomallos, and of Phrixus' sister, Helle.

Phrixus had told him that Chrysomallos was a hero. That he had returned to search for Helle but had died from exhaustion upon his return. Phrixus explained that he had removed the Golden Fleece from the Ram's body and that he brought it to show his grandfather and to honour Chrysomallos' bravery.

Aeetes was deeply moved by this gesture, and he welcomed Phrixus to his kingdom.

***

Phrixus fell in love with Chalciope, the king's eldest daughter. On his wedding day Phrixus gave his father-in-law the Golden Fleece as a thank you for making him so welcome into the royal household, and for the love he shared with his daughter, Chalciope who was now his bride. Legend has it that they lived many joyous years together, and that he became heir to King Aeetes' throne.

Poseidon was a guest at their wedding. He recognised the Golden Fleece, but kept his own counsel.

The king was deeply moved by the gesture, and he had a garden shrine built for his grandsons Golden Fleece. He hanged the Golden Fleece in a giant oak tree. He next posted two fierce fire breathing, brass hooved bulls, as guards and protectors of the fleece. Later, he acquired a dragon and he staked it to the tree to protect the fleece from thieves.

Ownership of the Golden Fleece altered Aeetes perspective. Over the years, he changed from being kind and benevolent ruler, to a king that was insecure and guarded.

***

Poseidon knew the truth about his son's fate, but chose to say nothing. Later that night, he visited the Golden Fleece alone. He held it with both hands and whispered. 'You deserved better my son. Then in hushed tones he added. 'I was sorry to learn that your short life ended in this way for you. I truly did have big plans for you.'

'In your honour my son!' he boomed in a godly voice. 'They shall never forget you.' He cast his hands toward the heavens and the constellation of the "Ram", now known as "Aries," came into the night sky for the first time.

***

Poseidon did actually rescue Helle from the sea and he saved her from drowning. He had originally planned to reunite the two, but he could not undo Chrysomallos slaying. He soon realised that he desired her, and so she became one of Poseidon's consorts. Sadly, she remained depressed about being separated from Chrysomallos, so as an act of kindness, Poseidon wiped her memory and renamed her Athamantis. Over the years they had two children, who were named Almops and Paeon.

For the most part, they were content. Sometimes, to amuse her children, Athamantis would make recognisable shapes from the oceans foam.

***

The nearest land mass to where Helle fell to her death is now known as Cape Helles. It is a rocky headland at the southwestern tip of the Gallipoli Peninsula near the western end of the Dardanelles in Türkiye.

***

A large asteroid was named Athamantis by astronomer K de Ball after its discovery in 1882

***

Many years later, Jason and his crew of Argonauts, which included the Gemini twins, Castor and Polydeuces, sailed the Black Sea in the mighty sailing ship "The Argo", in a magnificent quest to locate the Golden Fleece and steal it away from the Kingdom of Colchis.

To learn all about that adventure, you'll need to read another story.

***

The Greek constellations – Gemini, by Stephan De Jonghe is now available in paperback and eBook.

Novella one - the constellation Pisces

The story of Aphrodite and Eros, the Two Fishes.

Aphrodite is well known as the Greek goddess of love, romance, and sexuality. Aphrodite is also known to us as Venus, and the planet is named after her in her honour. This is the story of how Aphrodite came to be. Born in the ocean during a struggle between father and son, she was raised on an island. As an adult she was carried by Zeus to Mount Olympus to work and play with the gods and goddesses who lived there.

After a brief marriage to Hephaestus, she formed a steamy relationship with Hephaestus's brother, Ares and they had a son they named Eros. All her life, she struggled with the unwanted, yet amorous advances of the Titan monster named, Typhon. Eventually, she and Eros had to flee Mount Olympus to escape his wrath, and they eventually became the constellation of the Two Fishes known to us as the **constellation** *Pisces*.

Novella two – the constellation of Capricorn

The story of Pricus the Sea-Goat.

Pricus is an old sea-goat with a problem. He is regarded as the old man of the sea. The younger generation wants desperately to abandon the old ways and leave their ocean home to live a more adventurous life on the land. The sea-goats are able to morph from sea-goats into land goats when they emerge from the surf to walk on land. They quickly learn to morph into human form, and to their delight discover that they can have much more fun exploring the plethora of opportunities that await them. In their naivety they make many mistakes, some ending in tragedy. Pricus is desperate to save the younger generation from themselves, and so must become increasingly resourceful do so, and do so in a way that his solution remains permanent. His dedication to his own kind earns him his place as the constellation of the sea-goat, known to us as Capricornus or *Capricorn*.

Novella three -
Saturn's moon Pandora

The story of the first human woman.

Zeus, king of the Greek God's, commissions his son Hephaestus to craft the first human woman. Aided by Athena, he carefully researched the perfect form and then moulded her from clay He then painted and glazed her into the perfect woman. After being fired in his kiln, she was given the breath of life by the wind god Zephyr. She was named Pandora, being the bearer of the gifts bequeathed to her by the gods and goddesses of Mount Olympus. Her main purpose for humanity was to become the role model for all future human women. Zeus then commanded that she be properly trained so that she can navigate life's complexities. But her tutors do too good a job with her, and she becomes too powerful for a normal human life. Zeus became disillusioned with her, and he decided that she should be married off to a minor god, so that she'll do no harm to herself, or to others.

Pandora's story is so significant that she is honoured as *Pandora*, one of Saturn's moons.

Novella four - the constellation Taurus

This is the story of the Europa's meeting with Zeus as the white bull.

When Zeus, king and master of the gods and goddesses of Mount Olympus finds himself between wives he sets out on a desperate search for the perfect woman to marry. On a sunny field, set among spring flowers, on a stretch of land adjacent to the sea, he finds her. She is Europa, a gorgeous African princess. For Zeus, it becomes love at first sight. In his infatuation for this woman, he tries numerous times to impress her, and almost succeeds. Unfortunately for Zeus, his one true love is betrothed to another, and sadly for Zeus, a daughter must do her duty. Disguised as a magnificent white bull, he tries one last desperate attempt to win her affections.

The consequences of his quest for true love are celebrated as the constellation of the white bull, know to us as the *Taurus*.

Also commemorated in this story is the constellation *Draco*, known as Ladon the Dragon. Also featured is Laelaps as the constellation *Canis Major* or Greater Dog, and the Teumessian Fox as the constellation *Canis Minor* or Lesser Dog.

Novella five - the constellations Scorpio

The constellations Scorpio and Orion and the story of the scorpion verses the hunter.

Artemis is the goddess of the forests and of the hunt. She befriends a hunter named Orion. Their friendship is slowly progressing toward a blossoming romance when Orion boasts of his ability to wantonly kill all the animals that cross his path. Artemis is dismayed. Her policy is to only kill for food, to kill for pleasure is an outrage. She feels she must sacrifice her future relationship by stopping Orion from completing his boast. She manifests a giant scorpion and sends it to attack and destroy Orion. A massive battle ensues, and both are defeated, thus preserving animal life from indiscriminate killings. To celebrate the outcome and to remind us that all life is precious, their images were cast into the heavens as the constellation **Orion** and the constellation of the Scorpion known to us as **Scorpio**.

Novella six - the constellation Aries

The story of Chrysomallos the Ram and Helle.

Born from a union between Poseidon and Theophane on a remote island that was the home of a flock of sheep. They are interrupted by shepherds during copulation, so they disguised themselves as sheep to avoid the embarrassment that Theophane might suffer if their tryst became public knowledge. Their male child was born with the ability to morph from a human into a ram. From his mother, he has long golden hair, and when he becomes a ram, he has golden fleece. He has wings and the ability to fly.

He is named, Chrysomallos and is raised by his loving mother, Theophane. He eventually befriends the princess Helle who lives in a nearby kingdom. When their lives become perilous, Chrysomallos the flying, golden fleeced, ram comes to her rescue. His bravery is celebrated as the constellation of the Ram, know to us as *Aries*.

Novella seven - the constellation Ophiuchus

The story of Asclepius the serpentius or serpent bearer.

Asclepius was the son of Apollo. When Apollo had to rescue Asclepius from his dying mother's womb, he realised that he did not know enough about medicine and surgery, and so he set about discovering as much as he could. He later taught all that he learned to his son. Next, to further his education, Apollo decided that Asclepius would learn even more from the tutor Chiron. Through him he completed his training and went on to be the foremost authority on how to manage illness and repair injuries. His wife Epione and he had five daughters and three sons, and all became involved in the practice of medical treatments. The most prominent daughter was Hygieia and the practice of hygiene is named after her.

Both Apollo and Asclepius have been forever revered as the fathers of medical treatments and their names were included in the original Hippocratic Oath, that all medical practitioners swore upon when becoming formally registered to become doctors.

His dedication to healing the sick and injured was commemorated in the night sky as the constellation *Ophiuchus*. Many people who practice in astrology believe that Ophiuchus is the unrecognised thirteenth star sign.

Also featured is the constellation of **Serpens** or "The Snake." Who Asclepius witnessed bringing healing herbs to another snake who was sick, and this event started him on his discovery of benefits of medicinal herbs.

Novella eight - the constellations Cancer and Leo

The stories of Cancer and Leo and of Karkinos the giant crab, Zosma the Nemean lioness, Astron the hydra, Aquila the eagle, Sagitta the arrow, and the constellation named after Herakles the Demi-God.

The birth of Herakles was surrounded by controversy. Being the demi-god son of the King of all the gods, he found it difficult to live a routine life with his wife and children.

Herakles was persecuted by Hera for being her husband Zeus's illegitimate son, and so he was inflicted by incessant painful headaches. He was told of a remedy by the oracle in Delphi, but before he could be cured, it required him to agree to take on many incredible tasks which were assigned to him by the local king. By completing these labours, he should be able to go on to live a long and fulfilling life.

He later became immortal, and Herakles is forever remembered as a Greek Mythological hero for defeating the giant crab that became known as **constellation Cancer.** He also killed the man-eating lioness that became known as the **constellation Leo.** He then slew the serpent of Lake Lerna, which is now known as the **constellation Hydra.** Herakles used an arrow now known as the **constellation Sagitta,** to kill a giant eagle that became to be known as the **constellation Aquila or "The Eagle".**

Herakles was finally accepted at Mount Olympus and was honoured with the **constellation Herakles** also known as **Hercules.**

Novella nine - the constellation Gemini

The story of the twins, Castor and Polydeuces.

Leucippe was desperate to become a grandmother. Fed up with her son-in-law's lack of progress, she asked Zeus for his assistance. When Zeus arrived, he took the opportunity, and disguised himself as a swan, and then he did much more than just arrange for Leda to become pregnant.

The Spartan twins grew up to become skilled horsemen, hunters, warriors, and adventurers. They embarked on many journeys together and their adventures included sailing on the Argo with Jason on his quest for the golden fleece, being hunters at the Calydonian wild boar hunt, and fighting Trojans at Troy. It was their sister Helen, who was the central reason for that protracted war.

The twins were honoured by Zeus for their bravery and commitment to each other, and he cast their image into the night sky to be forever remembered as the constellation of the Twins, which is now known as *Gemini*. Also featured in this story is the constellation The Swan or *Cygnus*.

Novella ten - the constellations Virgo and Libra

The story of the Astraea the maiden and Themis the scales.

Astraea and Themis were both goddesses who were committed to advancing the living conditions of the humans who lived on the island of Thera. Along with other gods and goddess they believed that they would become the role models for all future human progress advancements.

However, the speed of their progress and their intentions to achieve self-determination worried Zeus. After inspecting the work and assessing all that had been achieved, he concluded that it must come to an abrupt end. And as every Greek immortal knows, when Zeus is determined and has made up his mind, nothing stops it his decision from happening. For Astraea the decision was devastating, so she cast herself into the night sky as "the maiden", forever watching in judgement over humanity as the **constellation *Virgo***.

Themis was later honoured for her balanced outlook on life, and is remembered as the scales as she evenly balanced out her reasoning and decisions. She is now known to us as the **constellation *Libra***.

Novella eleven – the constellation Aquarius

The story of Ganymede the water bearer.

Ganymede was adopted by a family of shepherds when he was found abandoned as a young child. He preferred his own company, and whilst good at caring for the sheep he was regarded as a misfit by his adopted family.

One day, as he is tending the sheep, he was spotted by Zeus, who flying past in his eagle form. Out of curiosity Zeus landed to meet the young man and became quickly enamoured with him. Ganymede found himself attracted to the powerful God and very much wanted to be with him. Zeus easily convinced the young man to give up his shepherding life and come with him to Mount Olympus.

Ganymede became Zeus's friend and lover. He took over the role of cup bearer during important civil functions from Zeus's daughter Hebe, as she had found love and married a Greek Hero. Ganymede quickly became fascinated with aqueducts and fountains, and he was responsible for improving the water quality and availability of clean drinking water to Mount Olympus's inhabitants.

His contribution is celebrated as the constellation of the "water bearer" now know to us as the **constellation Aquarius.**

Novella twelve – the constellation Sagittarius

The story of the "Archer" Crotus.

A water Naiad nymph named Eupheme was a demi-goddess of the Hippocrene freshwater spring near Mount Helicon. She was youthful, very beautiful, and powerful. She met and had a relationship with the God Pan, a Satyr, famous for playing the pipes was the god of shepherds, flocks, rustic musicians, and improvisation. Their romance led to the birth of Crotus.

Crotus was a Satyr and grew up to be like his like his father, preferring the company of muses. Most Satyrs preferred the company of Dionysus, God of wine, revelry, and debauchery, so Crotus was unusual in this way.

The muses were providers of inspiration to artists, musicians, poets, story tellers, artisans, entertainers, and dancers. They brought out the natural talents of those they inspired, and positively encouraged them to excel by pursuing their passions and striving for perfection in their chosen art form.

Crotus was also a great hunter, and many say that he invented the hunting bow. He was more popular as a musician and his most noteworthy contribution to performance music was the addition of rhythmic beats used to accompany the musician's musical score. He was also responsible for the introduction of a ritual applause to signify both pleasure from the performance and gratitude to the artist for their dedication to the composition and the quality of the performance. The act of giving applause was widely recognised as a significant motivator for artistic excellence.

Crotus was a mortal, and when he died, the Younger Muses petitioned Zeus to have his likeness immortalised as place in the night sky. Their petition was positively received, and, in his honour, he created the **constellation of the Archer** which is known to us as the **constellation Sagittarius.**

Novella thirteen – the constellation Centaurus

The story of the tutor Cheiron.

Cheiron was a centaur who became the tutor to many of the legendary heroes of Greek mythology. Unlike other centaurs, Cheiron was intelligent, civilised and very kind. He was the teacher of students that included Jason, Castor, Polydeuces, Asclepius, Peleus, and Achilles and he taught them philosophy, archery, hunting, medicine, music, gymnastics, and the art of prophecy.

His life ended tragically when he was accidently struck with a poisoned arrow by his close friend, Herakles. Herakles had loosed the arrow in an attempt to ward off marauding cruel centaurs who came to cause mischief to Cheiron, but in the confusion, Cheiron stepped into the path of the arrow and was stuck. His immortality prevented his death, but the strong poison caused him everlasting agony. He decided to surrender his immortality to Zeus so that he could pass into the underworld.

He was then commemorated as the constellation of the Centaur and is known to us as the **constellation Centaurus**.

The other Greek constellations

The other Greek constellations that may be featured one day in a novella include Andromeda, Ara, Auriga, Boötes, Cassiopeia, Cepheus, Corona Australis, Corona Borealis, Corvus, Crater, Delphinus, Equuleus, Eridanus, Lepus, Lupus, Lyra, Pegasus, Perseus, Piscis Austrinus, Triangulum, Ursa Major, Ursa Minor, and Argo Navis (now divided into Carina, Puppis, and Vela)

The stories of these constellations are a "watch this space" (literally)

Follicle Farm – A novel adventure

Follicle Farm – A novel adventure. (Fiction)

Follicle Farm is a comical and imaginative insight into organisational structure and behaviour of the trillions of cells that make up the microscopic world of every living person. It reveals how cells within the human body really think and how they, mostly, work well together. Bobby is a Mitochondria and he works as a humble Follicle Farmer. He, with millions of colleagues, are part of the amazing organisation dedicated to growing hair for the human male that they live inside of. Recently, Bobby made an important discovery when he learned how to reverse the effects of alopecia and greying hair. Now it's up to management to debate if they should use his technique.

Join Bobby as he travels the body, ably assisted by Banjo and Skip, as he meets and deals with other human cells in various systems throughout the body. Bobby quickly learns there is more to management than just servicing the body's needs. Cliques, quirks, politics, unions, and hidden agendas, all thrive in Bobby's world.

You'll share in his adventure of personal growth as he encourages other Follicle Farmers to utilise best-practises in growing quality hair.

This book is now available in Paperback or E-Book

Your concise guide to the meaning of life

This is a serious non fiction book which is designed to help people. Its main purpose is to assist you on how to gain insights on how to live a happier and more fulfilled life. It will give the you, the reader, instant benefits. It is peppered with many great quotes, many of them are my own. I've combined my interest in philosophy, sociology, psychology, and history to delve into the true meaning of life. The reader will not only understand why they are here, but how to make their experience more meaningful.

My main aim is to inspire readers into taking more control of how they make decisions that positively affect their achievements, successes, happiness, and therefore their well-being. The book is a summary of concise points that are easy to learn and apply to the readers life for an immediate benefit. It includes popular relevant quotes to re-enforce the messages and teaching. I have also included personal anecdotes that give real life and meaningful examples of how the material applies to all readers.

Topics include

- an explanation the main purpose for living.
- how to improve your relationships.
- how communication works and how to make it more effective.
- understanding your needs and desires and how to improve outcomes for yourself.
- understanding what motivates other people.
- how to exceed your own expectations.
- understanding your own personal legal, moral, ethical, and value system.
- improving your control over your emotions.
- understanding the concepts of faith, fate and fairness.
- and being better prepared for the final stages of your life.

This book is now available in Paperback or E-Book

Visit the website www.folliclefarm.com.au to learn more, or to purchase your paperback copy.